Ho**l**... Puppy Friends

Illustrated by Sophy Williams

stripes

Other titles by Holly Webb

The Snow Bear
The Reindeer Girl
The Winter Wolf

Animal Stories:

Lost in the Snow
Alfie all Alone
Lost in the Storm
Sam the Stolen Puppy
Max the Missing Puppy
Sky the Unwanted Kitten
Timmy in Trouble
Ginger the Stray Kitten
Harry the Homeless Puppy
Buttons the Runaway Puppy
Alone in the Night
Ellie the Homesick Puppy
Jess the Lonely Puppy
Misty the Abandoned Kitten
Oscar's Lonely Christmas
Lucy the Poorly Puppy

Smudge the Stolen Kitten
The Rescued Puppy
The Kitten Nobody Wanted
The Lost Puppy
The Frightened Kitten
The Secret Puppy
The Abandoned Puppy
The Missing Kitten
The Puppy Who was Left Behind
The Kidnapped Kitten
The Scruffy Puppy
The Brave Kitten
The Forgotten Puppy
The Secret Kitten
A Home for Molly

My Naughty Little Puppy:

A Home for Rascal
New Tricks for Rascal
Playtime for Rascal
Rascal's Sleepover Fun

Rascal's Seaside Adventure
Rascal's Festive Fun
Rascal the Star
Rascal and the Wedding

Contents

1   Timmy in Trouble   7

2   Harry the Homeless Puppy   129

3   Buttons the Runaway Puppy   253

www.hollywebbanimalstories.com

STRIPES PUBLISHING
An imprint of Little Tiger Press
1 The Coda Centre, 189 Munster Road,
London SW6 6AW

A paperback original
First published in Great Britain in 2015

ISBN: 978-1-84715-603-7

Printed and bound in the UK.

10 9 8 7 6 5 4 3 2 1

Timmy
in
Trouble

For Eddie and Jamie – keep writing!

Chapter One

"How's yours coming along, Katie?" Dad asked.

"I'm just thinking…" Katie doodled in the corner of her Christmas present list. A little dog's face, with big long ears and round, dark eyes. She smiled to herself. He was cute!

"Well, it's only four weeks until Christmas," Dad pointed out. "Both of your grans want to know what to get you as well, you know. You'll end up with socks, if you don't give them some ideas."

Katie's list wasn't very long. Just a couple of books, some new trainers and a mobile phone, which she knew she wouldn't get because her mum thought she was too young.

"Is that all?" her dad asked in surprise, looking over her shoulder.

Katie looked at him thoughtfully. Was now the right moment to ask?

Dad glanced over at Jess's list. Katie's older sister was sitting on the other side of the table, and her list was enormous. It was also very messy. "I can't read any of that!" he complained. "You'll have to copy it out, Jess."

Jess looked down at her paper and grinned. "It's not my fault. Misty kept coming and sitting on it, you know what she's like! I had to write around her."

Misty the cat stopped washing her paws when she heard her name, and looked at them all innocently. *Who me?* she seemed to be saying. She adored pieces of paper, and if anyone was writing, or reading a newspaper, she was never happy until she was sitting right in the middle of the page.

Jess leaned across the table to look at Katie's list, too. "You're not getting a phone," she pointed out. "Mum won't even let *me* have one. You can't only want a pair of trainers."

"Sounds like a nice easy Christmas shopping trip," Mum said, coming into the kitchen.

Katie smiled hopefully. She'd only put the phone on the list so her parents would say no, and then hopefully they'd be more likely to say yes to what she *really* wanted. "So I can't have a phone, then?" she sighed.

"Absolutely not!" her mum said.

"Oh," Katie said, crossing it out. She tried to sound disappointed, but it wasn't very convincing. "Well, there is one other thing…"

Her dad folded his arms, smiling at her. "I knew it! Go on, break it to me gently, Katie. What is it, an elephant?"

Katie smiled back. "Not quite. But … it is an animal." She took a deep breath. "I really, really want a pet."

Mum and Dad exchanged a thoughtful glance, and Jess stopped chewing her pen and sat bolt upright.

"A pet! We can't have another cat, what about Misty? She'd hate it."

Katie shook her head. "I know. I don't want a cat, I want a dog. A puppy. That's what I'd absolutely, definitely, more-than-anything like for Christmas. Please?" she added, smiling as sweetly as she could at her dad. She knew how much he loved dogs…

"I'm not sure it's a very good idea,

Katie," Mum said slowly. She looked at Misty, who'd gone back to washing herself. "Jess, please don't let Misty sit on the table. Her paws are dirty."

"They can't be, she spends the whole time washing them!" Jess pointed out. "Anyway, she'll just jump up again when you aren't looking, Mum."

Mum picked Misty up, and tickled her under the chin. "Not on the table, Misty," she said firmly.

Misty stared at her, waiting until she turned round. Then she leaped straight back up again. Katie, Dad and Jess giggled, and Mum peered over her shoulder and sighed. "I think I'll just pretend I didn't see that," she muttered.

"Mum, why isn't it a good idea?" Katie asked pleadingly. "It would be brilliant to have a dog. You can train dogs," she added persuasively. "I'm sure a dog would be better-behaved than Misty!"

Misty glared at Katie, then jumped on to Jess's lap. "Misty's very well-behaved," Jess protested, stroking her gently.

"Anyway," Jess continued, "I don't think Misty would like us having a dog. She hates dogs. Remember how cross she got when Meg from next door got under the fence? She hid up at the top of the apple tree for hours!"

Mum nodded. "I know. Misty might not be keen. We'd have to make a lot of extra fuss over her. And who'd look after this dog when the two of you were at school? Me, I suppose!" But she was smiling.

"Well, if we did get a puppy, we'd certainly have to be careful. We'd have to introduce the puppy to Misty slowly, so they got used to each other." Dad smiled thoughtfully. "I had a dog when I was your age. It was great fun – we went on lots of walks together, in the park and down to the woods. And now you're eight, Katie, I think you're old enough to help care for a puppy, feeding it and grooming it. Having someone else to look after would help you to be more responsible."

"You mean we *can* have a puppy?" Katie cried, jumping up excitedly and nearly knocking her chair over.

"No," Dad said firmly. "I mean we'll think about it. Not no, but not yes. We need to think it through very carefully, it's not something you can just decide in a moment."

But Katie had seen the wistful look in Dad's eyes when he was remembering those walks with his dog. And she was almost sure that really he meant yes.

Chapter Two

Dad refused to say anything else about dogs that weekend. Katie tried asking a couple of times if he and Mum had had time to think about it yet, but she didn't want to get on his nerves right now. She couldn't believe that they actually might be getting a puppy! She'd hoped, of course, but hadn't really expected them to say yes, or even half-yes. It was so exciting!

She spent ages on Sunday afternoon looking at her favourite dog websites on the computer, wondering what sort of puppy they might be able to get, and reading all the advice for new dog-owners. There was an awful lot to learn. Especially if you already had another pet, like Misty.

Katie dreamed of dogs that night. She was running through the woods with a gorgeous puppy, just like Dad had described. When she woke up she had a huge smile on her face, although she couldn't quite remember what the puppy had looked like. Brown and white, she thought vaguely, with big, floppy ears. But she could remember his happy, excited little bark, and the soft feel of his springy fur under her hand. It was a wonderful dream. And it might, just possibly, be about to come true!

She was still smiling as she wandered downstairs for breakfast, with her school uniform on all anyhow and her curly hair still full of tangles.

Mum took one look and sent her back upstairs again. "Brush your hair, Katie, for goodness' sake. And put it in bunches, you've got PE today, remember." She smiled. "I'd hurry up, if I were you. Dad and I have got something to tell you both!"

Katie raced back up to the bathroom. As she galloped up the stairs, she could hear Jess asking what was going on.

Less than two minutes later, Katie was back. Her hair was in bunches, although the bands didn't match and one was higher than the other. "What is it? What do you want to tell us?" she gasped, as she dashed into the kitchen.

Dad chewed a mouthful of cereal very, very slowly, and winked. He was obviously enjoying keeping them in suspense.

Mum shook her head. "Don't tease Katie, Gareth! It isn't fair!" She gave Jess a slightly anxious look as she said it.

"OK, OK!" Dad put down his cereal bowl, and beamed at Katie. "Yes."

"Yes? Really?" Katie jumped up and down excitedly and ran to hug her dad. "When? This Christmas? We're getting a puppy for Christmas!"

"But you can't!" Jess cried. She pushed her plate away and stood up. "You just can't, Dad! What about Misty? Katie can't look after a dog properly, anyway! And what about all those adverts on TV about not giving dogs as presents? *A dog is for life, not just for Christmas.* All those poor puppies get abandoned every year, it's wrong!"

Dad nodded seriously. "I know, Jess, sit down. You too, Katie. I haven't finished explaining."

Jess sat down, looking worried, and Katie sat too, though she was so happy she could hardly keep still.

Dad leaned towards them. "We're not giving you a puppy for Christmas, Katie—"

Katie's eyes opened wide with horror.

"But you said…"

"We are getting a puppy, but he or she will be a family dog. Like Misty's a family cat, Jess. You're right that Katie's a bit too young to have all the responsibility of a dog by herself." Dad smiled at Katie. "There's a lot of looking after, so don't worry, there'll still be plenty for you to do."

Katie felt like butting in and saying that actually, she was sure she *was* old enough, but she decided it was best not to.

Mum leaned over to touch Jess's hand. "Try not to worry, Jess. We know we're going to need to be really careful when Misty meets the puppy. We'll all do our best to make sure she doesn't get upset."

"And the puppy won't arrive at

Christmas, Katie," Dad added. "We're going to try and get one before Christmas, if we can, or maybe afterwards. Christmas is just too busy – it's not a good time to bring a new dog into the house. Mum and I have agreed we'll look around for someone with puppies for sale locally. Happy now?" Dad beamed.

Katie nodded blissfully, but Jess was staring at the table, twisting her fingers together. "I still think Misty's going to hate it," she muttered. She looked anxiously over at Misty, snoozing by the kitchen radiator on her favourite pink blanket. It had been Jess's when she was little, and Misty had adopted it.

"What sort of dog shall we get?" Katie asked, ignoring her grumpy big sister.

She wished she could remember the puppy in her dream better.

"Nothing too big!" Mum said quickly.

"But not too small, either. We want to be able to go on some good long walks." Dad sounded as though he was really looking forward to it. "Maybe a terrier? An Airedale, they're great dogs, really friendly."

"I've always liked pugs," Mum said thoughtfully.

"The ones with the squished-up faces?" Katie asked, giggling.

Mum nodded. "I like the way their tails curl up," she said, smiling. "What about you, Katie? This was your idea. What kind of dog would you like?"

Katie thought back to her dream.

"What sort of dog has long ears?" she asked, wrinkling her nose as she tried to remember more. "A brown and white puppy with long ears. I dreamed about one like that last night."

Jess sniffed, as though she thought that was silly. "You can't get a dog because of a dream."

"Why not?" Mum asked gently. "Katie's been thinking about it a lot, Jess. That's probably why she dreamed about a puppy."

"Maybe it was a spaniel?" Dad suggested. He got up and disappeared into the living room. They could hear him muttering to himself as he searched the bookcase, and he came back with Katie's dog sticker book. "Was he anything like this, Katie?"

Katie took the book and gasped with delight. There he was. A little brown and white dog, staring impishly out of the page at her, his eyes bright and alert. "A cocker spaniel," she murmured, reading the caption. "Oh, yes! I mean, I'd love any dog – even one with a squished face, Mum! But I'd really, really love one of those…"

Chapter Three

A couple of days later, Katie was kneeling on the window seat in the living room, waiting for her dad to come home from work. As soon as she saw him walking down the road, she shot out of the front door and raced towards him.

"Hurry up, Dad, you're so late! I've been waiting ages!"

Her dad looked at his watch. "It's only six o'clock, Katie, that's my normal time. Has your mum made a special dinner or something? What's the rush?"

"Oh, well, it feels later," Katie said excitedly. "We have to have dinner really quickly – we're going to see some cocker spaniel puppies! Mum found out about them, the breeder only lives twenty minutes away!"

Luckily, Dad was as excited as she was, especially when he heard that Katie had seen pictures of the puppies on the breeder's website, and one of them was brown and white, exactly like the one in Katie's book. They both finished dinner ages before Mum and Jess, and Katie glared at Mum when she started making a cup of coffee afterwards.

"Mu-um!" she wailed. "We have to go! We said we'd be there by now!"

Jess was still slowly finishing her yoghurt, making each spoonful last, and Katie scowled at her, too. "You're doing that on purpose!" she said accusingly. "You don't even like yoghurt all that much, you don't have to scrape the pot clean!"

"Go and put your coat on, Katie," Mum said. "We're obviously not going to get any peace until we go! Hurry up, Jess, you really are taking ages."

Jess huffed, but put the pot in the bin and went to get her coat, too. She looked like she was about to have a spelling test, not going to see a litter of gorgeous puppies.

29

"What's the matter?" Katie asked her in the back of the car. She was so excited about seeing the puppies, but Jess was sending out a black cloud of gloom right next to her. Katie couldn't ignore it. "Are you jealous?" she whispered. "You're being so grumpy."

Jess looked like she might snap back, but then she sighed. "No. I'm just worried about Misty, that's all."

"She might like having a dog to make friends with," Katie suggested hopefully.

But Jess looked doubtful. "We'll see," she murmured.

The puppies were just as lovely as Katie had imagined they would be.

The breeder's house had a conservatory at the back, which was being used as a puppy room. Katie could hear the puppies squeaking and yapping as soon as they got in the front door.

Mrs Jones, the breeder, laughed at Katie, who was hopping up and down with impatience as Mum and Dad followed her into the hall. "Come and see them," she said, leading everyone through to the conservatory. The door was blocked off with a board at knee height to keep the puppies in their own space. They were tumbling around all over the room, while their mother watched them from a comfortable cushion.

Katie couldn't see the little brown and white puppy she'd loved from the website. "There was one brown and white boy puppy in the photos. Has he gone already?" she asked anxiously.

Mrs Jones looked around the room. "Goodness, where has he gone? He's the cheekiest of them all. Ah!" She smiled, and pointed. "Look! See that big cardboard tube?"

Katie nodded. The tube was wriggling, and as she watched, a little brown nose appeared at one end, followed by some stubby whiskers and a pair of sparkling dark-brown eyes. The brown and white puppy popped out of the tube and stared curiously at the visitors.

"Oh, he's gorgeous!" Katie giggled.

"Do you want to go in and play with them?" Mrs Jones asked.

"Yes, please!" Katie said eagerly.

"Are they happy with strangers?" Dad asked.

"They're quite friendly," Mrs Jones replied.

"Well, remember to be really gentle, Katie," said Dad.

Soon Katie's whole family was sitting on the floor, with puppies sniffing and licking and climbing over them. Even Jess couldn't resist the cuddly little things. There were only five puppies, but there seemed far more as they all wriggled and darted around so quickly. The brown and white puppy was definitely in charge – or at least he thought he was. Katie watched him hopefully. She really wanted to pick him up, but she didn't want to scare him.

The puppy gave her an interested look. She smelled nice. Very friendly.

Katie gently held out the back of her hand for him to sniff, and he crept up to her, his tail wagging gently. He sniffed her fingers, then butted them lovingly with his nose.

"Your nose is cold," Katie whispered. She ran her fingers over his silky, domed head. His fur was so soft.

The puppy closed his eyes blissfully, and rested his chin on Katie's knee. That was *very* nice.

"He's a beauty," Dad murmured. "What do you think, Katie? Is this the one?"

Chapter Four

There was a lot to do before Katie and her family could bring the puppy home. Katie, Jess and their mum went to the pet shop on the way home from school the next day, with a long list. Katie had brought all her pocket money with her, although she didn't have an awful lot left after buying Christmas presents. It certainly wasn't enough to buy everything she wanted to get for their new puppy.

"Katie! Come and choose a collar and lead," Mum called from the counter. Katie left off choosing between a squeaky fish and a bright-orange nylon bone, and ran over.

"What colour do you think?" Mum said thoughtfully. "This blue one is nice."

Katie nodded. "Ye-es… But don't you think he'd look gorgeous with a red collar? It would show up really well against his brown and white fur." She lifted out the bright collar and held it up.

Mum added the red collar and lead to the pile on the counter – a sleeping cushion, a big bag of puppy food, and food and water bowls. "Did you find a toy for him, Katie? And where's Jess, did she want to get anything?"

"She's choosing a Christmas present for Misty. I'll get her. And I've *nearly* decided which toys."

Katie managed to limit herself to three dog toys, and five minutes later they were walking home, laden down with bags.

"There's one thing missing, girls. We still need to think what we're going to call the puppy. Ow, this food is heavy!" Mum shifted the bag to her other hand.

"I've been thinking about it!" Katie hitched up the big purple cushion they'd chosen for the puppy to sleep on. The man in the shop had said some puppies liked to chew baskets, so cushions were better. "I think he really looks like a Timmy. Sort of cheeky but cute."

She looked anxiously at Mum and Jess.

"Timmy… Yes, I like it," Mum said.

Jess just shrugged. Even though she'd enjoyed cuddling the puppies at Mrs Jones's house, she still wasn't sure that they should actually get one. "It's OK," she muttered.

Back at home, Katie wandered round the kitchen, trying out the cushion and bowls in different positions.

"Katie, I'm not cooking with a dog cushion in front of the oven," Mum pointed out. "Try by the radiator, that'll be nice and warm."

Katie pushed Misty's blanket out of the way, and stood back and looked at the cushion. "That's perfect!" she declared happily.

Misty prowled in from the hallway

and stopped. Someone had put a big purple cushion exactly in her favourite sleeping spot. She stalked over and stared up at Katie accusingly.

"Hi, Misty!" Katie bent down to stroke her. "Look, this is where your new friend's going to sleep. He's a puppy, and he's called Timmy. He's so sweet, and I bet you'll love him!"

Misty climbed on to her fleecy pink blanket and sat down, squishing herself in beside the vast cushion. She glared at it disapprovingly. What was going on?

Katie didn't notice. She was looking at the calendar on the wall and wishing it wasn't so long until they brought Timmy home. "Another three whole days till Saturday!" she sighed. "That's ages!"

The brown and white puppy gazed thoughtfully up at the window. It was only very slightly open, but the most delicious smells kept floating through it. Fresh air and frosty ground and general outsideness. It smelled *wonderful.* The puppies weren't allowed outside yet, as they were too young, but the brown and white puppy was desperate to explore. Where were all those delicious smells coming from?

He looked round. His brothers and sisters were snoozing in their basket, and their mother was half asleep, too. If he went for a little wander now, probably nobody would notice…

Mrs Jones had left the window open

to air the room, but she'd carefully made sure it was only open a crack. Not that the puppies were big or strong enough to get up on to the windowsill, of course! They were far too small for that.

The puppy looked up. Beneath the window was a chair. It was still too high for him to reach, but next to that was the old cardboard box Mrs Jones had given them to play with. If he climbed on to that first, maybe he could jump on to the chair, and then to the window?

He scrambled on to the box, tiny claws scrabbling. Then he made the next hop on to the chair. Hmmm. It was still a long way to the windowsill. But...

"Oh, you naughty little thing!" Mrs Jones was half-laughing, half-cross, as she rescued the brown and white puppy, who was standing on the chair seat, his paws on the back, staring up at the open window hopefully. "You could have really hurt yourself. And I suppose you were making for the window. I'd better shut that." She smiled. "I think your new family ought to call you Rascal. You're going to be a real little handful!"

On Saturday morning, Katie woke up early, with a wonderful feeling of excitement inside. She was still sleepy, and it took her a couple of minutes to work out why she was feeling so happy. It was the first day of the Christmas holidays, but there was something more… Then she remembered. They were getting Timmy today! She bounced out of bed, and flung on her clothes.

She clattered downstairs, wondering where everyone else was. Misty stared at her reproachfully as she banged the kitchen door open, then turned round on her blanket and settled herself down with her back to Katie.

Katie was aching with impatience by the time the rest of the family got up.

She couldn't understand how Dad could sit there with the paper, and drink a cup of coffee so slowly.

"When are we going to *go?*" she wailed, standing in the kitchen door with her coat on.

"It only takes twenty minutes to get there in the car," Mum pointed out.

Katie frowned. "But it takes at least five minutes to get *in* the car! It's rude to be late, Mum, you're always saying so."

"Well, that still leaves us half an hour." Dad folded up the paper. "Anyone else want more toast?"

"OI I!" Katie groaned, and stomped out of the room.

At Mrs Jones's
house, the
puppies
were
playing
a fabulous
game with

the big cardboard tube. It was only just wide enough for them to get inside now, and they were scrabbling through it, nipping at each other's tails.

Suddenly, there was a scratching, scuffling noise from inside the tube as the brown and white puppy shot out of one end. He shook his ears to unsquish them, then trotted hopefully over to Mrs Jones. "What is it, boy? Oh, there's the doorbell." She smiled down at the puppy. "Did you hear the car? Someone special's coming for you!"

When Mrs Jones answered the door, Katie had to stop herself dashing into the house and hugging the puppy – she was already thinking of him as Timmy. But she knew she mustn't. He was only little, and he probably wouldn't remember who she was. She would have to be really calm and gentle. But it was so hard when she was this excited!

Katie walked into the living room, digging her nails into the palms of her hands. Would Timmy even remember her?

The puppies were all standing by the conservatory door, watching to see who was coming. Suddenly, there was a piercing squeak of a bark, and a small brown and white ball of fur hurled itself at the board across the door, scrabbling madly. Two little white paws clawed their way over the top, and Timmy flung himself over the board, making for Katie as fast as he could. He knew that girl! She was the one who'd cuddled him!

"Oh my goodness!" Mrs Jones exclaimed. "None of them has ever done that before." She hurried forward. "Is he all right?"

Timmy was shaking himself dazedly – it had been a long way down for such a small dog – but then he barked again and ran to Katie.

Katie knelt down and hugged him to her lovingly. "Oh, Timmy. You remembered me!"

Chapter Five

Mrs Jones had given them a special box for carrying Timmy home. Katie was a bit disappointed, as she'd been looking forward to cuddling him in the car, but Mum said it might be dangerous if he wriggled out of her arms. He'd feel safer in the box.

Katie wasn't so sure. She hated hearing the snuffling, whimpering noises that Timmy was making behind her seat. He didn't sound happy at all.

"So when we get home, we're going to let Timmy out into the kitchen, girls, that's the plan," Mum reminded them. "He needs to get used to the house slowly. Remember he's only been used to staying in the puppy room. The whole house would be a bit daunting for him. And then we need to introduce him to Misty very carefully."

"Can I show him my bedroom?" Katie asked hopefully.

"I wouldn't just yet," Dad told her, as they turned into their road. "For a start the mess would probably give him a heart attack…"

Katie grinned. That was true. Timmy could quite easily get lost in there. As soon as the car stopped, she struggled out of her seat belt, her fingers clumsy with excitement, and gently lifted Timmy's box out of the back. She could feel him skidding about inside, even though she was walking so slowly and carefully. "We'll get you out in just a minute," she whispered. "You can see your new home!"

Katie carried Timmy into the house, and put the box down on the kitchen floor, kneeling beside it. Then she undid the flaps that held it together. Timmy stared up at her, puzzled by his strange, dark journey. But then he recognized Katie, and gave a pleased little whine, scrabbling at the cardboard with his claws to show her he wanted to get out.

"Come on, Timmy!" Katie lifted him out, and cuddled him lovingly. He was staring at her, his big, dark eyes bright and interested. Then all at once he reached up and licked Katie's chin, making her splutter and giggle.

"Well, I don't mind if you do that, but I wouldn't do it to Mum," she whispered to him.

Timmy gazed at her lovingly. He was a bit confused about what was going on – his brothers and sisters weren't here, and nor was his mum, but if he was going to get cuddled and played with, maybe it would be all right.

He wondered if there were any other dogs here. He couldn't smell them, but there was another smell, a different smell that he didn't recognize…

"How's he doing, Katie?" Dad had come in from the car. He and Mum and Jess had been chatting to the lady next door, and telling her about their new arrival.

"I'm just about to show him his cushion and his food bowl," Katie explained. She walked round the kitchen with Timmy, holding him up to see out of the back door. Then she put him gently down next to his cushion. "This is where you're going to sleep, look."

Mum came in holding Timmy's collar and lead. "Don't forget these, Katie.

Remember what the website said – we need to keep him on the lead in case we have to stop him chasing Misty."

"Oh, yes!" Katie bent down and fastened the bright-red collar around Timmy's neck. "Very smart!" she said. She clipped on the lead and Timmy looked at it in surprise. What was this? Oh, a lead, like his mum had.

He sniffed at the big, purple cushion, and sneezed.

Dad laughed. "It probably smells a bit clean. Don't worry, Timmy, it'll be nice and doggy in a couple of days."

Just then, Jess came in, carrying Misty. She'd gone to fetch her from upstairs. Misty spent most of her time snoozing on Jess's bed.

Timmy was delighted. He peered

up at Misty, his whiskers twitching.
So that was what the interesting smell
he'd noticed was! A friend! He danced
clumsily over to her on his too-big
puppy paws, and barked cheerfully to
say hello. Katie followed, holding his
lead and watching
them cautiously.

The fur on Misty's back stood up on end, and her tail fluffed up to twice its normal size. She hissed warningly. *Stay away!*

"Timmy..." Katie said anxiously, but Timmy wasn't listening. He had no experience of cats, so he didn't recognize Misty's warning for what it was. He just wanted to say hello to this big, fluffy animal.

Misty hissed again, then yowled and spat, her ears laid right back against her head.

Timmy stared at her, feeling very confused. Then he backed up a little. He didn't understand what was going on, but he could tell now that something was wrong. He looked up at Katie and whimpered, asking for help.

"I told you she'd hate it!" Jess said accusingly to Mum. "Oh, Misty no!" Misty had jumped out of her arms, and was prowling across the kitchen towards Timmy.

Katie was just stooping to pick him up, when Misty pounced, and swiped her paw across Timmy's nose – not very hard, just enough to make it clear she really wanted him gone.

Timmy howled in surprise and dismay. His nose did hurt, but it was more the shock of it that upset him so much. He'd played rough and tumble games with his brothers and sisters, but no one had ever scratched him before. He buried his nose in Katie's jumper, as she picked him up, and snuffled miserably.

Misty hissed at him triumphantly, her fur still bristling.

"That was so mean of Misty!" Katie cried angrily. "All he did was try to say hello, and she clawed him! His nose is bleeding!" She snuggled Timmy close and glared at Jess and Misty.

"Maybe we should put Timmy's cushion in the utility room to start off with," Dad said worriedly, looking at Timmy's nose. "I think it's a bit much for Misty to get used to all at once."

Jess folded her arms, and stared at the ceiling. "I told you this was a bad idea," she said. "Misty hates dogs, and this is her home. It's *never* going to work."

"Well, now it's Timmy's home, too!" Katie snapped back. "Misty's just going to have to get used to it."

Katie sat up on her bed in the dark, her duvet wrapped round her shoulders, listening anxiously as Timmy let out another mournful howl. Everyone had agreed that he would stay in the kitchen and the utility room at first, so he could get used to the house gradually. It was what all the dog books and websites had suggested, especially as Timmy was still learning to ask to go outside if he needed to. Mum really didn't want him messing up all the carpets.

Mum and Dad had been careful to keep Misty away from Timmy for the rest of the day, after their fight. For tonight they'd put a litter tray in the hall, and Misty was sleeping on Jess's bed, as she always did. Katie had begged her parents to let Timmy sleep in her room, too, just for his first night, but Mum had said definitely not.

Timmy just didn't understand why he couldn't explore the rest of the house. Katie had stayed in the kitchen almost all that day, playing with him, and cuddling him, but Timmy had still been curious about what was going on everywhere else.

That cat was allowed to go wherever she liked, but he had to stay in, except when he was taken into the garden to do a wee. It didn't seem fair. And when she wanted to be in the kitchen to eat her food, he had to go into the utility room! Why couldn't he eat with her? She might even have leftovers.

But the worst thing was that now they'd all gone to bed. He had to sleep in the kitchen, and he was all on his own! It was so lonely! Where was everyone?

He howled so much that Katie just couldn't get to sleep. She sat there listening to the sorrowful wails from downstairs, and eventually she couldn't bear it any longer. She crept out of bed, wrapping her duvet round her like a cloak and trailing it along behind her. Mum might have said Katie absolutely must not have Timmy in her room, but she hadn't said anything about not sleeping in the kitchen with Timmy, had she?

Timmy was sitting on his cushion, staring anxiously into the darkness. Like all dogs, he could see well in the dark, but he wasn't used to being all alone – he never had been before. What if Katie never came back? He didn't want to be on his own for ever!

Timmy whimpered again, and then stopped. He could hear footsteps, and an odd swishing noise. What was that?

He looked worriedly at the door, hoping it wasn't something horrible. Maybe the cat was coming to be mean to him again. In his mind, she was about twice her real size, and her tail was enormous. Maybe that was what the strange noise was... Timmy whined nervously.

Katie hitched up her trailing duvet and gently pushed the door open. She called softly to him. "Timmy? Hey, sweetie!"

Timmy heaved a massive sigh of relief and trotted over to her.

"Ooops!" Katie giggled. "I just walked into a chair! It's so dark."

Timmy woofed in agreement. Dark, and lonely. He gazed hopefully up at her.

"Look, I've brought my duvet. I've come to keep you company for a bit. You're used to having your mum to sleep with, aren't you?" Katie curled up next to Timmy's cushion, and he snuggled gratefully on to her lap. This was much better.

Katie smiled down at him, as he dozed off into a deep puppy sleep. He was hers, at last! The kitchen floor was chilly, and she had pins and needles in her toes, but she didn't care. It was worth it.

Chapter Six

Katie's mum came downstairs on Sunday morning, and found them both curled up together, Katie with her head on Timmy's cushion, and him snuggled under the duvet with her.

"Katie! I thought you were still in bed! Actually, I was surprised you weren't up and playing with Timmy already." Mum sighed, as she poured

Katie some juice and filled Timmy's food bowl. "I should have known."

Katie grinned. "Sorry, Mum. He was so lonely. I listened to him whining and crying for ages, and then I just couldn't bear it any longer."

"The thing is, now he'll expect you to do it again tonight." Mum watched as Timmy wolfed down his breakfast. "You can't sleep on the kitchen floor every night, Katie!"

Katie wriggled her shoulders. "I know, this floor's really hard. Honestly, Mum, I won't do it again. I think he was just miserable the first night, that's all."

Katie was right. Timmy had never been left alone before, and he hadn't been sure that anyone would ever come back for him. Now he knew that Katie and the rest of the family weren't far away, and he'd see them in the morning, he didn't mind being alone so much.

In fact, on Sunday night, he was so worn out from playing in the garden with Katie for most of the day, that he curled up on his cushion and fell asleep almost as soon as she went to bed. He didn't bother with even one little howl.

A couple of days later, Katie's parents decided that Timmy had settled in so well that they could let him explore a bit further.

"Just downstairs, mind," Dad said. "There's so much stuff he could accidentally damage upstairs. Imagine if he started chewing your mum's shoe collection. She'd never forgive him!"

Katie nodded, though she wished she could have Timmy in her room. Still, she was really looking forward to curling up with him to watch TV in the living room.

"Come on, Timmy," she called, standing by the kitchen door and patting her knees. "Come on, boy!"

Timmy looked at her with his head on one side. He wasn't quite sure what was happening. He wasn't allowed out of that door, was he? He'd been told no when he tried before. He pattered slowly over to Katie, then turned and looked at her mum, waiting to see if she'd tell him off.

Mum laughed. "It's OK, Timmy. Go on, go with Katie."

Timmy woofed with excitement, and trotted happily into the hallway. New things to smell! He worked his way curiously along Katie and Jess's school bags and wellies, which were by the front door, then poked his nose into the living room. Jess was sitting on the sofa reading a magazine, with Misty on her lap.

Over the last couple of days, Katie and Jess and Mum and Dad had very carefully kept Timmy and Misty apart. They wanted to give Timmy time to settle down, and Misty needed to get used to the idea of a dog in the house.

Misty spent as much time as she possibly could in Jess's room, only coming into the kitchen to bolt down her food – with one watchful eye on the utility room door the whole time. She would then shoot out of the cat flap, and rely on Jess letting her in the front door when she wanted to come in again. Now she looked up at Timmy, and hissed.

"Oh, Misty!" Katie sighed. "Don't be so grumpy."

Timmy had almost forgotten his first meeting with the cat. He was only very little, and he was naturally friendly. He assumed everyone else was, too. He bounced over towards Misty and Jess, his tail wagging, and yapped excitedly at her. Misty shot on to the arm of the sofa and growled, her back arching.

Timmy's tail drooped, and he looked

round at Katie. He was only trying to be friendly. *Why doesn't she like me?*

"Keep him away from Misty," Jess said irritably. "He's upsetting her."

"Mum said we could watch TV," Katie said. "There's a safari programme on; I thought Timmy could watch it with me. Anyway, Misty and Timmy have to learn to get along. If we can just get them used to being in the same room, that would be really good."

"I suppose..." Jess muttered. "Just keep an eye on him, though!"

For the next half-hour, Misty glowered from the arm of the sofa, her tail twitching warningly, and Timmy shot her curious, sidelong glances from the armchair, where he was curled up on Katie's lap.

Gradually, Misty started to relax, and after a while she dozed off on the sofa arm, with one eye half open.

Timmy sat quietly for a while, but

soon he began to feel restless. He slipped down from Katie's knee, and went exploring. This was much more exciting! Katie was half-watching him, but the little lion cubs on the programme were so cute!

Timmy sniffed his way round the room, investigating behind the Christmas tree and sneezing at the dust under the big bookcase. He even managed to wriggle under the sofa. It was dark, and it smelled interesting. He could pop his head out from underneath as well, and then hide again, which made Katie giggle. It was a good game.

He crawled the whole length of the sofa, and poked his nose out at Jess's end. There was an interesting fluffy thing there, dangling down, and twitching gently.

Timmy was mesmerized. It went to and fro, waving at him. The fluffy thing was like one of the toys Katie had given him, a furry rat that squeaked. Maybe this one would squeak, too, if he bit it? He wriggled a little further out from under the sofa, just as Katie realized she hadn't seen him for a minute or so.

"Where's Timmy? Is he behind the sofa? Oh, Timmy, no!"

And Timmy pounced on Misty's tail...

Chapter Seven

Misty shot up in the air with a screech, and Timmy howled in shock – he hadn't expected the fluffy toy to do *that*... He peeped nervously from under the sofa just as Misty raced out of the room. Why was she so upset? Perhaps it was *her* fluffy toy?

"Oh, Timmy..." Katie said worriedly. She was trying to sound cross, but she couldn't help a tiny smile – Misty had looked so funny, like something out of a cartoon, as she'd leaped into the air.

"I'm telling Mum!" Jess snapped. "He did that on purpose, and you weren't watching him!" Then she ran after Misty.

Katie picked Timmy up. "Oh, Timmy. That was her tail. I don't think you knew that, though, did you? You didn't do it on purpose, I know you didn't. Our plan to get you and Misty to like each other isn't going very well, is it…"

And things got worse and worse over the next week. Rather than Misty and Timmy getting used to each other as time went on, Misty just got more and more furious about her peaceful home being invaded. She tried as hard as she could to keep away from Timmy, but she couldn't escape from him. It seemed that wherever she went, there he was, too.

Timmy didn't understand that Misty wanted to be left alone. She kept running off upstairs whenever he tried to play with her, and when he tried to follow he got told off.

He was allowed out on his own in the garden now, though, and he thought he'd had a stroke of luck one afternoon when he found her snoozing on the garden bench in a patch of winter sunlight – she couldn't dash away up the stairs now! But she raced up to the top of the apple tree and snarled at him, while he barked hopefully. But eventually, he gave up and ran over to Katie, who was calling him in.

Back in the kitchen, Timmy lay quietly on Katie's lap, even though she bounced his squeaky ball for him. His ears were drooping, and he rested his nose on his paws, gazing sadly at the back door.

"You really want her to play with you, don't you?" Katie sighed. "I think Misty's a bit old for playing, Timmy."

Timmy heard the worry in her voice, and rubbed his head against her arm lovingly.

But Katie was right. Misty was an old cat, and stubborn. She didn't like new things, and she found it so strange and upsetting having Timmy around that she didn't even want to eat properly any more. Besides, her food was in the kitchen, where he was. It was easier just not to bother. As the days went by, she started to look thinner.

A few days before Christmas, Timmy was curled up on his cushion, feeling bored. Katie had left him in the kitchen, explaining that she had to go upstairs and wrap presents in her room, because they were a secret, and no one was supposed to see. Timmy still wasn't allowed upstairs, but she promised she'd be back soon.

Katie had shut the kitchen door when she went upstairs, but Timmy had been practising, and he could claw it open unless it was shut really tight.

Timmy hooked his claws into the crack and scrabbled until it clicked open. Then he trotted cheerfully out. He was so clever! Katie had been ages. He was sure she wouldn't mind if he went to find her, would she?

Timmy headed for the stairs, and suddenly felt a little less clever. They were very big. He almost couldn't see the top. But he knew Katie would be up there. He could smell her, and as a tracking dog, his sense of smell was excellent.

He heaved himself up on to the first step, which wasn't too difficult, except there were a lot more of them before he got to the top. Timmy sighed and set about the next step. It took him ten minutes to get all the way up, and he nearly went back to his comfy cushion several times.

But the exciting new smells upstairs soon made him forget how hard it had been to get there, and he set off snuffling along the carpet. Ah! An open door! Maybe Katie was here. No, it didn't smell like Katie. But there was Misty, curled up asleep on the pink bedcover. Timmy trotted eagerly into the room. He was delighted to see her. If he woke her, perhaps she would play with him. He stood up with his front paws on the edge of the bed and licked Misty's nose. He could only just reach.

Misty was sleeping peacefully, knowing *that dog* was downstairs and she didn't need to worry. Then she woke up with a sudden fright.

He was right there! There, in Jess's room! Was nowhere safe any more? Misty leaped off the bed, and raced across the room, looking for a way to escape. Timmy was whining, trying to show her he was friendly, but all Misty could see was Timmy in the one place she'd felt was safe. Desperately she clawed her way up Jess's curtains, and up on to the top of the wardrobe.

The scuttling and barking brought Jess running upstairs; Katie rushed in after her.

"He's not meant to be in here!" Jess yelled. "Get him out of my room! Misty, it's OK, come on down, puss, puss…" She turned back to Katie, who was standing by the door, looking horrified. "Go on, get him out!" she cried angrily.

Timmy flinched back. Jess was so angry with him, and Misty was cowering on top of the wardrobe… It had all gone wrong! He'd only been trying to be friendly. And now he was in trouble again!

Katie scooped him up and hurried downstairs. "Oh, Timmy! What were you doing up there? You mustn't chase Misty, it's mean!"

Katie sounded cross, Timmy thought miserably. He sighed. He hadn't meant to be naughty.

"What's going on up there?" Mum was standing at the bottom of the stairs looking worried.

"Katie let Timmy get into my room, and now Misty's stuck on top of my wardrobe!" Jess yelled from upstairs. "Mum, we have to shut him in the kitchen so Misty can calm down, it's just not fair."

"Oh, Katie. He didn't upset Misty again?"

Timmy whined sadly as he heard another cross voice.

"Jess is right, Katie," Mum said firmly. "Put Timmy back in the kitchen, and make sure the door's shut tight. And hurry, Katie, we've got to finish off the Christmas shopping this morning, remember. We need to get going."

"But Mum, he doesn't really like being shut in…" Katie started to say, but Mum gave her a stern look, folding her arms. Katie sighed. "Sorry, Timmy. You have to go back in the kitchen. Stay here and be good, all right?"

Timmy watched, his big, dark eyes mournful, as she carefully shut the door. He was all alone, and everybody was cross with him. He howled miserably at the ceiling, then slumped on his cushion, listening to Katie and Jess and Mum in the hallway, getting ready to go out.

Timmy wriggled around sadly, trying to get comfortable. A piece of pink material was hanging on the radiator, and he knocked it down as he turned. It made him jump, as it fell

on to his cushion.
Timmy took it
in his mouth
to pull it out
of the way,
but he had
it tangled in his paws,
and it tore a little. This was fun…

The pink fabric was good to chew. It made satisfying tearing noises as he shredded it and shook it and rolled around the floor with it. He felt much better afterwards, but quite tired. It had been a busy morning climbing all those stairs.

Timmy fell asleep, covered in small bits of pink fleece.

A couple of hours later, Katie, Mum and Jess came back. Timmy could hear them outside the kitchen, and he scratched the door a few times, hopefully, but no one came to get him. He could hear Jess talking to Misty. *She* was allowed out. It wasn't fair. He trailed back to his cushion, and nibbled a bit more pink fleece.

"Where's Misty's blanket, Mum?" Jess called. "It's not in my room, and you know she likes to sleep on it."

"Oh, I washed it, Jess, it was so dirty. It's hanging on the kitchen radiator to dry," Mum said.

Timmy could hear Jess coming towards the door, murmuring to Misty. "It's all right, we'll get your blanket, then you can have a nice sleep."

As Jess opened the kitchen door, cuddling Misty, a guilty-looking brown and white puppy stared up at her, with shreds of pink blanket hanging out of the corner of his mouth.

Chapter Eight

Timmy lay on his cushion silently, only occasionally giving a sad little whine. Jess had been so cross, crosser than anyone had ever been with him before. She'd called him a bad dog, and lots of other horrible things. Even *Katie* had said he was naughty. He'd never heard her sound upset like that. And the worst thing was, they were right.

He *had* been naughty.

The kitchen door clicked open gently, and Katie came in, wearing her pyjamas. Timmy looked up at her sadly. Was she still angry with him?

"Oh, Timmy. I'm sorry we shouted. You didn't know, did you? But Misty's really upset, Timmy, and Jess is *furious*." Katie sighed. "I thought you and Misty would learn to get along, but it just isn't happening." She stroked his ears gently, and Timmy laid his nose on her knee, gazing apologetically at her.

Katie looked guiltily round at the kitchen door, and then scooped him up in her arms. "Come on. We're both too miserable to be on our own. Mum and Dad have gone to bed, so I'm going to sneak you up to my room. We've got to be really quiet, because if anyone catches us, we'll be in big trouble, OK?"

Timmy snuggled gratefully into Katie's arms, and she tiptoed upstairs. She tucked him down beside her, and Timmy felt happy for the first time since Jess had been so cross. At least Katie still loved him.

But the next morning, Jess flung Katie's bedroom door open, and rushed in, her face panicky.

Katie rolled over. "What is it?" she asked, too sleepy to remember that she ought to hide Timmy. Luckily, Jess seemed too distracted to notice him.

"Have you seen Misty?" she asked anxiously.

Katie shook her head, yawning.

"She didn't come back in last night! I was sure she'd be here this morning. She does stay out late sometimes, but never all night." She frowned at Katie. "You know why she's gone, don't you? Because of Timmy. He's driven her away, Katie!"

"That's not true—" Katie started to say, but Jess didn't let her finish.

"Of course it is! He eats her food, he chases her, he's bitten her tail, and now he's chewed up her most special thing! I'm just surprised she didn't leave before!"

Katie sat up in bed, carefully covering Timmy with the duvet.

"Misty's just old and grumpy, and she's never been at all friendly to Timmy. She was the one who scratched him!"

"She's a cat, Katie! Cats don't like dogs! I told you and Mum and Dad that, and nobody listened, and now we've lost her. You were the one who wanted a dog in the first place. It's all your fault!"

"No, it isn't!" Katie yelled back, making Timmy tremble beside her. He hated shouting.

"It is, and stop trying to hide Timmy, because I know you've got him up here, and I'm telling Mum!" Jess stormed out, leaving Timmy whimpering.

"It's OK, boy," Katie muttered. "It'll be OK…"

But she wasn't at all sure that it would.

Katie and Timmy were in disgrace. Jess was still claiming that Misty had run away because of Timmy. Katie had to admit it was true, but he hadn't been naughty on purpose – he was just being a dog, a friendly, bouncy, messy puppy.

He hadn't meant to upset Misty!

Dad had called their vet to tell them that Misty was missing. Misty had been microchipped, so that if anyone brought her into the vet's, they could tell at once who she belonged to. But Mum and Dad were sure that she would be back soon.

"It's only been one night, Jess," Mum said at breakfast, putting an arm round her.

Katie sat on the other side of the table, feeling miserable. She was worried about Misty, too, and Mum had really told her off for having Timmy in her room. Now he was lying under the table, resting his nose on her feet. He could sense how upset everyone was, and it was horrible.

"She'll be back as soon as she gets hungry, Jess," Dad promised. "And it's the first morning of my holiday from work, remember, so I can help you look for her later if she doesn't turn up."

"It's only two days till Christmas!" Jess wailed. "What if Misty isn't back for Christmas Day?"

The problem was Misty didn't want to be found. She was miserable, and she wanted to hide away from people, and especially from *dogs*. When she had seen her precious blanket in pieces all over the kitchen floor, she had known that she couldn't stay in the house any longer.

Misty had left home, and she wasn't coming back. Not while the dog was still there. She had plodded dismally through the garden, crawled under the back fence, and set off down the alleyway that led to the main road. She wanted to be far away, and by the time Jess had finished shouting at Katie and Timmy, and raced after her, Misty had gone too far to hear her frantic calling.

Misty liked being outdoors. She was good at hunting – she loved to give Jess mouse presents – and she adored sunbathing in the garden. Only now it was freezing, and she could smell snow in the air. And it felt different being outside all alone and knowing that she couldn't just slip back in through her cat flap to be safe and warm again.

She spent the night huddled under a garden shed, a few streets away from her own house. It was horrible; still, she couldn't go back. But when she woke in the morning, hungry and stiff with cold, Misty wished that Jess was there to cuddle her, and open one of her favourite fishy tins for breakfast. Maybe she should go home, just for some food, then she could leave again, after she'd seen Jess…

Misty crawled out of the grubby little den she'd found, and sniffed the air anxiously. Home was – which way?

In a sudden panic, Misty leaped on to the top of a garden wall, looking worriedly around. She didn't know! She had been so desperate to get away yesterday that she hadn't tried to remember. Now all the gardens looked the same, and none of them was hers...

Chapter Nine

It was the saddest Christmas Day ever. The whole family was sitting in the living room, with the Christmas tree lights on, trying to be enthusiastic about presents. Carols were playing, and it looked like a perfect Christmas scene. Even Timmy had tinsel round his collar. But there was a cat-shaped hole, where Misty should have been perched on the back of the sofa, waiting to pounce on the crackly wrapping paper. Everyone was thinking about her.

"Your turn, Jess!" Mum said brightly.

Jess stared at the pile of parcels in front of her as though she wasn't really seeing them. She was holding a plastic packet in her hands, with a picture on it that looked very much like Misty. Katie looked over at her miserably. She'd been with Jess at the pet shop when she'd bought it – the luxury cat "chocolates" that were meant to have been Misty's Christmas present.

Tears started to seep out of the corners of Jess's eyes, and Mum sighed. "Let's leave the rest of the presents till later."

Dad stood up. "Come on, Katie, it's time for Timmy's best Christmas present!"

Katie nodded. She and Dad had planned ages ago to take Timmy for his first walk on Christmas Day. Katie had been looking forward to it ever since they got Timmy – they'd had to wait until he'd had all his vaccinations before he could go out and meet other dogs. They were going to take him just as far as the park near Katie and Jess's school, so as not to tire him out too much. "Timmy, walk, come on!"

Timmy raced to the front door, leaping excitedly around Katie's legs, squeaking and whining with delight. They were going out! Katie had his lead. He'd seen other dogs at his old house with them on, and he knew it meant a walk.

"Timmy, calm down! Sssh! Look, if you don't keep still, I won't even be able to get it on you!" Katie was half-laughing, half-cross. She was trying to clip the lead to Timmy's collar, but he kept licking her hand and barking, and then rushing to scrabble at the door.

Katie's dad grabbed his coat, and stuffed a handful of papers into his pocket.

"What are they?" Katie asked.

Her dad sighed. "Just some more posters. I promised Jess."

"Oh..." Katie nodded. Suddenly the excitement about their first walk faded a little. Jess had papered their neighbourhood with "lost" posters over the last couple of days, but no one had called to say they'd seen a fluffy grey cat. Katie wondered if she should go and ask Jess if she should take some too, but Jess still wasn't speaking to her.

Timmy looked up at them, and whined again. He felt the change in Katie, that suddenly she wasn't happy any more. He guessed it was because of Misty – everyone was unhappy about her. He missed her, too, even though she would never play with him. He hung his head sadly.

Jess wandered into the hallway, followed by Mum, who was looking at her watch. "I need to sort out the roast potatoes and things. You go with them, Jess. You can't sit around all day. I know you don't want to, but honestly, getting some fresh air will make you feel better."

"Oh, Mum, no…" Jess murmured.

"I mean it, Jess. Go and get your coat on." Mum gave Jess a quick hug, and a gentle push in the direction of the door. "Go!"

Even Jess trailing along in a miserable cloud couldn't stop Timmy dancing about and winding his lead round Katie's legs as they headed out of the front door. There was so much to see, so many delicious new smells. He was sure there must be at least a hundred other dogs on this street, he could smell them all! Timmy suddenly stopped, nearly tripping Katie up with his lead.

"I think Timmy might need some obedience classes soon," Dad said, laughing.

Katie tried to coax him to move, but Timmy wasn't listening. He'd had a brilliant idea. He could smell all those dogs, so clearly. He was *good* at smelling things. So maybe he could sniff out Misty! He bounded ahead, his nose busily at work. There were lots of cat smells, too…

Misty was hiding out behind a big, smelly bin, in a tiny yard behind a row of shops on the way to Katie and Jess's school.

It was horrible. There were rats, and although Misty liked to hunt mice, the rats were not the same thing at all, they were big and frightening. She was huddled inside a tattered cardboard box, and every so often a rat would scurry past. The only good thing about the yard was that there was quite a lot of food around, although it wasn't as nice as those special tins Jess gave her.

Jess... Misty got up and turned round, anxiously. She didn't want to think about Jess. She missed Jess so much, but Jess didn't care about her any more. Jess had let a dog into the house. Even into Misty and Jess's room. That wasn't Misty's home now. Jess didn't love her any more.

But what was she going to do? Another rat scuttled past, baring its teeth at Misty. She couldn't stay here, but she had no idea where to go. *I need a new home,* Misty thought miserably. *But I don't want one. I want my old home back!*

And I'd even share it with that dog, if it meant I could still be with Jess...

Timmy was the only one enjoying the walk. He danced about, snuffling and scrabbling happily as they reached the shops, and all those interesting smells. There were definitely cats here, too.

Jess was silent, trudging along with her head down – except when they happened to see a cat, when she'd look up hopefully, then sigh and stare at the pavement again.

"I think it's going to snow." Dad was looking up at the sky. "The clouds have got that yellowish look. And it's certainly cold enough. I'm freezing. Shall we turn back, girls?"

"Mmm. Come on, Timmy." Katie tugged gently on his lead. But Timmy wasn't listening. He was straining forwards against the lead, looking excited. Then he turned and gazed anxiously at Katie, and uttered a sharp, urgent bark.

Can you smell what I smell?

"Timmy, we're going home, come on, boy."

No! Not now, we have to go this way!

"Tim-my!" Katie's voice was starting to sound cross.

Timmy looked worriedly up at her. How could he make her understand? He had a horrible feeling she wasn't going to. But he was sure he recognized that smell and he had to investigate… Timmy gave Katie an apologetic look with his big, dark eyes, and moved a step towards her, loosening his lead.

"Good boy, Timmy," Katie said in a relieved voice.

Then Timmy jumped back suddenly, dragging his lead out of Katie's hand, and dashed away down a little alley, following that familiar scent. Now where was it coming from...?

Katie stared down at her hand for a second, as though expecting the lead still to be in it. Than she raced after Timmy, calling anxiously to him.

"Katie! Timmy!" Dad had been staring at the snow clouds and looked back just in time to see Katie vanishing down the alley, too.

Timmy bounded into the little yard, trailing his lead, and stopped, looking around. Now he was here, there were lots of other smells, too – old food, and strange animal smells that he wasn't sure about. But yes … there was a definite hint of Misty's scent, as well. She was this way. He trotted over to the bins, poking his nose between them hopefully. Yes! There she was! Curled up in an old cardboard box, and staring fearfully back at him.

Timmy barked for joy. He'd found her! He called excitedly for Katie to come, then rushed at Misty. He was just so glad to see her. Now everyone would be happy! He licked Misty's nose lavishly, and she shuddered and hissed, backing further into the box. Timmy stepped back doubtfully. *Aren't you pleased to see me?*

Misty gave a sad little mew. Where *was* Jess? Maybe the dog could show her? She edged slowly out of the box, the fur on her spine slightly raised. *Don't lick me again,* she was telling Timmy. *But I'm not cross. Yet.*

Katie skidded into the yard, calling anxiously. "Timmy! Timmy, where are you?" She spotted his red lead, trailing out between the bins. "Oh, Timmy, are you eating something horrible?" She ran over, squeezing herself between the bins, and Timmy stared up at her proudly.

Look! I've found her! he barked.

"What is it?" Katie asked, peering a little reluctantly into the box. She had a horrible feeling Timmy had found something yucky. "Misty! Oh, Misty!" Katie whirled round. "Jess, Jess, come here, quick!"

Jess and Dad were just following them up the alley. "You've caught him," cried Dad. "Thank goodness."

"Yes, but look!" Katie picked Timmy up and hugged him lovingly. "Jess, come and see!" She stood back so Jess could get to the box. "Timmy's found her. He must have sniffed her out. That's why he ran off. He's so clever."

Jess dropped to her knees beside the box. "Misty!" she whispered.

Misty shot out of the box and Jess swooped down and picked her up.

Misty snuggled into Jess's coat, purring so hard her sides were shuddering.

"Katie, he found her!" Cradling Misty in her arms, Jess turned to her sister and Timmy. "I can't believe it…"

Timmy reached out from Katie's arms, wriggling and wagging his tail happily, and amazingly, Misty didn't snarl or hiss at him. She shut her eyes slightly as he licked her nose. She didn't look as though she was enjoying it, but she let him.

"They're friends!" Katie said in amazement.

Misty glared at her, as if to say, *Don't push it…*

But it was true. And above them, the first Christmas snowflakes were starting to float gently down.

"Misty, Timmy, turkey!" Katie laughed at Misty and Timmy, both standing eagerly by their food bowls. "Just a little, look, it's your Christmas dinner."

"Get on and eat yours, Katie," Mum

said. "Dad's nearly finished."

"Don't worry, I'll be having seconds," Dad said with his mouth full.

Jess wasn't eating very much either. Both girls just kept stopping and staring happily at Misty and Timmy wolfing down turkey.

"I hope Misty likes her new blanket," Katie said, ignoring the roast potato she was waving around.

"I bet she will, look, she's about to try it out. It's a gorgeous present, Katie." Jess smiled at her, and Katie grinned back. It felt like the first time in weeks that Jess had smiled so easily at her. The angry wall between them seemed to have just crumbled away.

Misty prowled thoughtfully over to the new pink, fleecy blanket that lay neatly by the radiator. Katie had bought it weeks ago on a trip to the pet shop. She'd seen how old and tatty Misty's blanket had become, and had decided it was the perfect Christmas present.

Misty walked round it a couple of times, then graciously stepped on to it, testing it with her paws. She lay down, the picture of a comfy, turkey-fed cat, and purred.

Timmy finished licking the last possible taste of turkey out of his bowl, and gave Misty's bowl a quick lick just in case she'd left any. He sighed happily. Then he trotted over to Misty's blanket, and gazed hopefully at her.

Misty gave him a resigned look. *If you must,* she seemed to be saying.

Katie and Jess watched, holding their breath, as Timmy whined eagerly, and snuggled down next to Misty, putting his nose next to hers.

Misty put a firm paw on one of his long, curly, brown ears. Clearly, if Timmy was on her blanket, he had to keep still.

Timmy looked up at Katie lovingly, and yawned. Two minutes later, both cat and puppy were fast asleep.

Jess put her arm around Katie's shoulder, and Katie smiled. It was a perfect Christmas after all.

Harry the Homeless Puppy

For Robin and William

Chapter One

"Beth, we need to go now," her dad told her gently. They didn't have much time before they needed to leave for the airport.

Beth didn't answer. She just stroked Harry's soft white head and chestnut-brown ears. She couldn't stop the tears dripping down her cheeks. The puppy jumped up, placing his paws on her shoulder, and licked them away. "Oh, Harry, I'm going to miss you so much. I don't want to say goodbye," she whispered.

Her voice was so sad that Harry's curly tail stopped wagging. What was Beth talking about? It didn't sound good. He hoped they could leave this place soon. It was too noisy, and it smelled odd. There seemed to be lots of other dogs here, he could hear them barking and growling and whimpering. He wanted to go back to his nice home.

"Here's his basket, and his toys," Beth's mother said, putting them into the pen. "I'm sorry but we really do need to go, Beth; we have to set off for the airport soon. It's going to be so exciting, isn't it?"

Harry watched his basket, his favourite red rubber bone and squeaky fish being put into the wire cage. Beth squeaked the fish for him a couple of times, then rubbed her hand across her eyes. Harry gave a puzzled whine, looking up at Beth with his big, brown eyes. What was going on?

"Oh, Mum, he knows something bad is happening," Beth said, as she got to her feet.

"Don't worry," the girl from the shelter said gently. She was called Sally and she seemed nice, but Beth wished she'd never had to meet her. "He'll find a lovely home really soon, I'm sure. He's such a sweet little dog. Puppies are always easy to rehome, and Jack Russells are a popular breed."

Beth nodded, wiping her tears away with her sleeve. She supposed she ought to be glad about that – she certainly didn't want Harry to be here at the shelter for ages, all miserable in a little run. But she didn't want anyone else to have him either! He was hers.

She'd only had him for two months,

when her dad broke the news to her that his company was sending him to America for three years. At first it had seemed so exciting, going to live in New York, but almost at once she'd thought of Harry. Would he like it there?

And then Dad had said he couldn't come. That it would be too difficult with quarantine, and they would be living in a city flat that wouldn't be suitable for a dog. Harry had to stay behind, and since they had no one to leave him with, he had to go to the shelter – a home for unwanted dogs. Which didn't seem fair, because Beth did want him, very much.

"We'll write to you, to let you know when Harry's settled with a new owner," Sally promised. "Really soon. I know he's going to find a lovely home."

Beth wanted to shout out that he had a lovely home, but she nodded, and her dad led her out, which was good, because she was crying so much she couldn't see.

Harry whimpered, calling after her and scrabbling at the wire door. Beth was crying! There was something wrong, and she was going away from him. He howled for two hours, and then he was so exhausted he fell asleep.

When he woke up, she still hadn't come back.

"Oh, just look at this one," Grace said longingly. "A Labrador. Isn't she gorgeous?"

Mum smiled at her. "We haven't the room, Grace, you know that. Even though she is beautiful. Lovely eyes."

"Maybe a small dog, like a Jack Russell, then!" Grace started frantically scanning through the shelter website to see if they had any smaller dogs. "They're those cute little terrier dogs that used to hunt rats. They're really clever. And small! We've got room for one of those, definitely." Grace looked hopeful.

"No, we haven't. And you'll need to get off the computer soon, Gracie, I have to get on to the estate agent's website again, and see if any more flats have come up." The Winters were looking to move at the moment, as there just wasn't enough room for them all in their current flat, especially now Grace and her brother Danny were getting older.

"It's no use, Gracie." Danny sighed, as he squeezed behind the computer chair to go and make some more toast. The computer was squashed into one corner of the kitchen. "I've been trying to convince Mum and Dad to get a dog for years."

Mum frowned at him. "Don't you start, Danny. You both know we just haven't got the space. It's not fair to shut a dog up in a flat, even a little one. If we had a garden flat, maybe. But not on the seventh floor!"

Grace nodded. She knew it really, but every so often she managed to convince herself it wasn't true, just for a minute. She went back to stirring her cereal, imagining running through the park with a gorgeous black Labrador or a bouncy little brown and white Jack Russell scampering beside her. If they were moving anyway... Was it too much to hope for a flat with a garden? She licked her spoon dreamily.

"Don't get rice pops on the keyboard, Grace!" Mum warned.

"Hey!" Danny had paused behind Grace's chair with his plate of toast, and was leaning over her shoulder. "Gracie, look! Mum, come and see!"

"I'm never going to get on to my computer," Mum muttered, coming over to look at the screen "Fairview Animal Rescue Shelter. You're still on the dogs' home website? Danny, haven't we all just agreed we can't have a dog?"

"Yes, but look. Our Fantastic Volunteers! People who help at the shelter." He grabbed the mouse and clicked on the link. "Look, they get to walk the dogs!" Danny beamed at Grace. "We could do that, couldn't we? I know we can't have our own dog, but we could borrow some. It would be like having lots of dogs!"

Grace practically pushed her nose up against the screen. There was a big photo of a hopeful-looking dog, with a lead in its mouth. Bonnie, she was called, apparently. "Could we do it, Mum?" she asked eagerly. "The shelter's not far from here. Only a couple of streets away, on the other side of Fairview Park."

"Sounds like a good idea to me." Dad had walked in, and was staring at the computer now, too. "Anything that gets you out in the fresh air and not watching TV is good news. Does it say wwhen they're open? I'll take you over there later, if you like."

Danny scanned the page. "We're always looking for more volunteers," he read. "Please drop into the shelter!"

Grace smiled up at Dad delightedly. "You really mean it?" she breathed. She hadn't really expected to be allowed a dog, and this was much, much better than nothing!

Harry was lying in his basket, with his nose shoved firmly into his blue cushion. It smelled like Beth's house – his house – and it shut out the smells of other dogs. He couldn't understand why Beth had left him here, and why she hadn't come back. Beth had brushed him and fed him and loved him. She had run into the house to find him and play with him as soon as she got home from school. What had gone wrong? He hadn't been naughty, he was sure.

He could still hear the other dogs barking and whining, however hard he tried to bury his head in the cushion. But then he heard the sound of footsteps. Slowly, he crept out of his basket, and went to peer through the wire door of the pen. Maybe Beth was coming back? She might even be waiting for him out there! He sprang up against the wire hopefully, and from further up the corridor Sally turned round to look at him.

"Hey, Harry…" she said very gently. "You decided to come and see what's going on, did you?"

Harry's ears went back, and his tail sagged again. Beth wasn't there. Just that woman who smelled of other dogs. He slunk back to his basket, and Sally sighed. She hoped Harry wasn't going to have a really hard time.

Harry thought miserably about home. It felt like the sort of time he'd normally be curling up at the end of Beth's bed. His basket was usually only for daytime naps; he always slept with Beth. She'd probably have given him one of his favourite biscuit bones, too. He sighed, and snuffled sadly. She would come back, wouldn't she?

Chapter Two

Grace and Danny went to school round the corner from each other, Grace in the juniors and Danny at the secondary school. So Danny usually walked Grace home, except on Tuesdays when Grace had ballet. But today Mum was meeting them so they could all go to the shelter, and be properly registered as volunteers.

They'd gone on Saturday, but it had been really busy, and the staff had asked them to come back in the week, so they could meet the dogs when everything was less hectic.

"Oh, where is she?" Grace swung her school bag impatiently.

"She's not even late yet! We were finished early for once," laughed Danny. "Hey, which dog do you want to take out? I really liked that big lurcher on the website. He was great – I bet he runs like the wind!"

Grace smiled. "I don't mind. Any of them. Oh, look, there's Mum!" Grace ran over to her. "You were ages! Can we go straight there?"

Mum laughed. "Yes, but I just want to stop at the supermarket for a few things, OK?" She winked at Danny.

"Mu-um!" Grace's expression was tragic.

"She's kidding you, Gracie!" said Danny. "Honestly, you're so easy to wind up. Come on, let's get going."

Grace, Danny and Mum stood in the shelter reception, waiting for Sally, the manager, who was going to show them around. There was a constant noise of dogs barking and howling.

"You get used to it after a while," Mandy the receptionist said, smiling. "Think how happy you'll be making them, taking them out for walks. And it's not only walking. With some of the dogs it's just about companionship, a bit of playing or stroking. I'm afraid some of them have been badly treated, and we need to help them to trust people again."

"But none of them are dangerous?" Mum asked anxiously. "I wouldn't like Danny or Grace to be with any dogs that might bite."

"No, no." The receptionist shook her head. "Volunteers only take out dogs we trust completely." She grinned at them. "The only thing you need to worry about is not getting too attached! I've got three dogs from here, the ones I simply couldn't resist! You just have to remember that all the dogs are going to be rehomed eventually, or we hope so anyway. So don't let yourselves get too fond of them, will you?"

Grace peeped through the glass door, looking at the dogs peering back at her from their runs. How could she not fall in love with them all?

"Grace, did you hear?" Mum said gently. "Don't get too involved!"

Grace turned back and nodded. She would try...

The shelter wasn't too busy, so Sally took Grace and Danny and Mum round to meet some of the dogs they'd be able to walk. There were so many – Grace was torn between being glad there were lots of dogs for her to get to know, and sad that they all had no homes of their own. It was heartbreaking when the dogs jumped up at the doors of their pens, their tails wagging desperately, licking her fingers, clearly begging for her to love them and take them home.

"Oh, this one's gorgeous." Grace knelt down in front of one of the wire-fronted

runs to look at a little brown and white Jack Russell. "He's only a puppy!"

Harry looked up hopefully. Grace's voice sounded a little bit like Beth's. But his ears flopped back again when he saw her – just another girl. He turned round in his basket so he didn't have to look at her.

Grace gave him a surprised look. All the other dogs had been desperate for attention, and had wanted all the stroking and cuddling they could get. But this little puppy seemed to want them to go away!

"This is Harry," Sally explained. "He's our newest arrival. He was left with us a week ago, by a family who were moving to America quite suddenly. The girl he belonged to was about your age, Grace. She was really sad to leave him."

"Oh, wow," Grace murmured. She could imagine. Harry looked really young. The other girl couldn't have had him for all that long before she had to give him away.

"He looks pretty miserable," Danny

said, crouching down to get a good look at Harry in his basket.

Sally nodded. "Yes, he's really missing Beth, his old owner. He is eating, but not much, and he won't respond to any of us when we try to cheer him up. I think he's still hoping that Beth's coming back for him."

"That's so sad," Grace said, her voice wobbling. "I wish there was something we could do to help."

Sally looked at her thoughtfully. "Harry isn't ready to go out for walks yet, Grace. If you wanted to spend time with him, it would have to be here at the shelter. Probably just sitting with him in his run, letting him get used to trusting another person. It's sad, but we just don't have the time for that very often, with so many dogs to look after."

Grace looked up at Sally, her eyes shining. "But I would love that!" she said gratefully. "Mum, is it OK? You don't mind if I stay here while you and Danny walk your dogs?"

"Well, as long as it's all right with Sally..." Mum said doubtfully.

"Honestly, you'd be doing us a favour," Sally assured them. "We're short-staffed, and we've all been feeling really bad that no one's had time to work with Harry yet. But Grace, don't expect too much to happen at once, will you? It might be a long, slow job. Poor Harry's really moping."

Grace nodded, looking at Harry's smooth little back, as he lay curled into a ball in his basket. His nose was tucked under his paws, as though he was trying to shut out the world. She would take it really slow.

"I'll let you into the run, then just sit down quietly to start with, not too close to him," Sally told her. "Then I'm afraid it's just all about waiting. See what he does. But if you spend some time with him every time you come, hopefully it will help him a lot. I'll make sure I stay close to check you're both doing OK." She opened the door for Grace, and Grace slipped inside, trying to be as quiet and unfrightening as she could.

Harry raised his head suspiciously and glared at her. It was that girl again. What was she doing in his run? He huffed crossly through his nostrils, and

Grace tried not to giggle, it was such a funny little noise. She leaned against the wall of the run, and watched Harry, as he turned himself away and snuggled sadly into his basket again. It wasn't quite what she'd imagined, sitting on the floor just looking at a dog, instead of racing round the park. But Harry was so little, and his face when he first looked up at her had been so hopeful, and then so terribly sad. Grace wanted so much for him to be happy again and sat there quietly until her mum and Danny returned.

Harry had always been a friendly dog when he lived with Beth, but he liked his own space, too. He didn't really enjoy being cooped up with a lot of other dogs. And he hated being shut up in a run. However hard the staff tried to exercise all the dogs, they had to stay in their runs for a lot of the day. As for the noise – Harry was a sensitive little dog, and the sound of barking made him want to hide under his cushion.

What made it worse was that other people kept bothering him. He was taken out of the run and given to them to hold. He wished they would just leave him alone so he could wait for Beth to come back and get him.

When was she coming back? He was still hoping that she would, but he was getting less sure every day.

That first day, Harry hadn't even looked at Grace. She wanted to go to the shelter on Tuesday, but she had her ballet class. But on Wednesday, when Grace visited, Harry actually stood up in his basket and leaned over to give her a considering sniff. Hmm. So it was her again.

On Friday she was back, so he licked her fingers, just to be polite. When she went, he watched her walking down the corridor. She smelled nice, and he wondered whether she would come again. On Saturday, he sat up in his basket when she opened the run, and when she crouched down beside him, he put his paws on her knee, positively encouraging her to stroke him.

"Oh, Harry..." Grace breathed delightedly. He was pleased to see her!

Harry hadn't been planning to make friends with the girl, but she was quiet and gentle, and she reminded him of Beth. It was nice to be stroked and petted again, and told what a lovely boy he was. He was still waiting for Beth to come back, of course, but there was no harm in letting this nice girl – Grace, the others called her – make a fuss of him.

The next Monday, Sally walked past Harry's run to see him curled up in Grace's lap while she stroked his ears. Grace was staring down at him with a little smile on her face. She was imagining that Harry was hers, and that they weren't at the shelter, they were sitting on the grass in her garden, a lovely big garden, just right for a dog to play in. None of the flats that they'd seen in their house-hunting had had gardens, but this was only a dream, after all…

"You've done really well with him," Sally said, smiling.

Grace jumped slightly – she hadn't noticed Sally coming. Harry grumbled a little when she moved, and turned himself round to get comfy again.

Sally watched him, looking pleased. "You've got a great feeling for animals, Grace. You've been so patient, and it's really paid off with Harry. We'll start trying to introduce him to more visitors now, I think. We'd really like to rehome him soon."

Grace only nodded. She couldn't trust herself to say anything. She didn't want Harry to be rehomed yet – then she'd never see him again.

Grace frowned at the knitting pattern. She was trying to make a little teddy for Harry to have in his basket, but knitting was a lot trickier than it looked when her nan did it. She sighed. She had a feeling that it wasn't going to look like the picture, but then Harry would probably chew it to pieces anyway. She just really wanted him to have something to remember her by. Visitors to the shelter kept saying how cute he was, and she was sure he was going to be rehomed soon. Grace sniffed, and a tear smudged the crumpled pattern.

"Grace," Danny called round the door. "We've got to go and look at this flat with Mum and Dad."

Grace frowned. Her room at the

moment was more like a cupboard, but she liked it, even if there wasn't enough space for a desk and she had to do her homework on her bed. It was comfy like that, anyway.

The new flat was really nice, with a much bigger room for Grace. She could imagine all her dog posters up at last, with all that space, and loads of shelves for her tiny china animals and her books. But it was a second-floor flat – with no garden.

"So what did you think?" Dad asked, as they were walking back home. "I really liked it."

Mum nodded. "Me too. Lovely kitchen. And your room was great, wasn't it, Grace?"

Grace shrugged.

"What is it?" Dad asked. "Didn't you like it?"

"I'd much rather have a tiny

bedroom, and a garden, so that we could have a dog. I really would. I don't need a big room, honestly."

"She's right," Danny put in. "A garden would be brilliant."

Mum sighed. "I know how much you two want a dog, and I've been really impressed with the way you've worked so hard at the shelter. But I still wouldn't feel happy leaving a dog alone all day. We'll have to think about it."

But she gave Dad a thoughtful look, and flicked through the list of flats that the estate agent had given them. Maybe they could find something…

Chapter Three

Harry had started to look forward to
Grace's visits. She usually came after
school, so at about half-past three he
would find himself standing by the
door of his run, sometimes with his
paws up on the wire, watching out for
her. That Friday afternoon, almost two
weeks after he'd first met Grace, Harry
woke up from a nice snooze in his

basket, and stretched out his paws. Now, why had he woken up? Was it food-time? No… Ah. It was Grace time. She should be coming to play with him soon.

"Oh, he's lovely! What a gorgeous little dog!"

A voice floated over to him, but it didn't sound like Grace. Harry blinked, still a little sleepy, and peered across the run. A young woman was looking at him, and Sally was with her.

Sally opened the run to let the woman hold Harry. He allowed her to pick him up, but he kept peering over her shoulder, looking out for Grace.

"He's been with us a couple of weeks now. He's a lovely puppy, but he's been missing his old owner. She had to go overseas. He's cheering up a bit now, but any new owners would have to take it slowly with him. Really take the time to build a relationship. And you know that Jack Russells are very energetic? They really need a lot of exercise."

The woman nodded. "I'll definitely go home and talk it over with my husband. I'll let you know very soon."

She waved goodbye to Harry as she walked down the corridor back to the reception area, and Harry wagged his tail delightedly and woofed. The woman smiled, thinking this was all for her – she didn't realize that Grace was just walking through the door behind her. She went home thinking what a sweet, affectionate little dog Harry was. He'd obviously taken to her.

Grace gave the woman a worried look as the door swung shut. Not another person admiring Harry! Everyone who came to the shelter seemed to think he was really cute. Grace had a horrible feeling that Harry would be going to a new home soon.

"Hey, Grace! I'm making some coffee; do you want some juice? And there's a packet of chocolate biscuits, look, I splashed out. Fancy one?" Sally waved the packet at Grace as she walked past the kitchen on the way to see Harry the next day. On Saturdays Grace usually played with Harry, and then tried to spend some time with any other dogs that the staff thought needed fussing over. Sally had asked her to help with a couple of other dogs who were quite shy and needed someone patient.

"Chocolate biscuits! Yes, please!"

Grace leaned against the kitchen door, nibbling her biscuit. She couldn't take it with her, the dogs would all want to share it, and chocolate was not good for dogs at all.

"You're doing really well with Harry, you know, Grace. It's made a big difference to him, you being here." Sally stirred her coffee thoughtfully. "You're going to miss him when he goes to a new home, aren't you?"

Grace nodded, her mouth full of biscuit. "Mmmf."

"Now that he's so much friendlier, I don't think it's going to be all that long before he goes. He's such a sweetie. Just keep it at the back of your mind, OK? I don't want you to be upset, that's all."

Grace stared into her orange juice. "I know…" she said at last. "I won't be upset. Really." She told herself that it was true, she'd always known that Harry would be rehomed. But deep down, she knew that she'd been secretly pretending that he was hers.

"Anyway, I reckon you could take him for a real walk today, if you fancy it?" Sally grinned as Grace nearly hugged her. "Watch it with the juice! I think he's ready. Danny's here, isn't he? Your mum's happy for you to go out if he's with you, isn't she?"

"Yes." Grace nodded excitedly. "I'll tell him."

Sally smiled. "It's OK, I'll find him. You go and put Harry's lead on. I should think he'll keel over with excitement. He just hasn't been getting enough exercise. Jack Russells really like a couple of hour-long walks every day."

Sally was almost right. As soon as Harry saw his lead, he started jumping up madly, leaping about and practically bouncing off the walls. He could jump easily as high as Grace's waist. She had to pin him under one arm to keep him still enough to put the lead on. "Calm down, calm down, silly boy," she murmured lovingly as he leaped up to try to lick her face.

Eventually she led him proudly out through the reception area, where Danny was waiting with Bella, the Labrador they'd first seen on the shelter website.

It felt so exciting, walking out of the shelter with Harry on his lead – it was a smart blue one that had been his when he belonged to Beth's family, and he looked lovely.

"Remember how I showed you, get him to walk to heel!" Sally called after them.

Grace looked down at Harry and grinned. Heel was a good idea, but... He was just so excited. She had to keep gently pulling him back every time he lunged after a strange smell, or wanted to chase a fluttering leaf.

Harry was blissfully happy. He hadn't been outside the shelter in so long – but as soon as he'd seen his lead, and heard Grace say walk, he knew exactly what it meant. He loved walks. He wanted to see everything! Every bee was a possible enemy that needed chasing, every leaf had to be checked out.

Grace was glad that Sally had reminded her to keep a really good hold on Harry when they passed other dogs. A huge Alsatian was walking beautifully to heel along the road towards them, and Harry spotted him even before she did. He barked mightily (just to show the Alsatian he wasn't scared, even if he was a little...) and tried his best to show that he was the bravest, toughest dog in the world.

The Alsatian's owner smiled at Grace. "You've got a real little character there!"

Grace nodded breathlessly. All her energy was going on keeping Harry under control. She hoped he wouldn't be like this with every dog in the park!

Luckily, he started to calm down after that, and by the time they were passing the shops he was walking quite nicely to heel.

"Hey, Grace, if I just tie Bella's lead on this hook, is it OK if I nip in and see if they've got the new skateboarding magazine?" Danny asked.

Grace looked doubtfully at Harry. He didn't look like he wanted to stop. "If you're really quick!" she agreed.

"Brilliant. Back in a minute." And Danny disappeared inside the newsagent's. Bella sat down patiently and didn't seem to mind waiting, so Grace bent down to pet Harry.

"Hi, Grace!" Someone was calling. Grace looked round to see her friend Maya from ballet coming down the road with her sister. "I didn't know you had a dog! What's his name? Can I stroke him?"

Grace blinked. "He's called Harry," she said slowly. "Yes, of course you can stroke him, he's very friendly." She knew she ought to tell Maya that Harry wasn't actually hers, but she just didn't want to… It was so nice to pretend that he really belonged to her. Harry was being so good, sitting and letting Maya pat him. Grace was so proud of him! And his good behaviour was mostly down to all that time she'd spent with him – so why shouldn't she let Maya think that he was hers?

"Come on, Maya, we've got to go," Maya's sister told her, and Maya stood up reluctantly.

"Grace, could I come over again one day, and play with you and Harry? He's gorgeous, you're so lucky!"

Maya had come over to tea a couple of times before, and they'd had a great time. But what was Grace supposed to say now? If Maya came round, she'd know that Grace didn't really own Harry.

Grace looked down at the floor. "I'll have to ask my mum," she mumbled.

Luckily, Maya's sister was in a hurry. "Come on, Maya, now," she said, heading off down the road.

"Um, see you at ballet!" Grace called, as Maya hurried off after her sister.

Maya was calling something back to her, but Grace pretended not to hear. She just hoped Maya didn't think she was being unfriendly. And what was she going to say to her at ballet if she asked again about coming over?

Maybe she should have told Maya the truth after all...

Chapter Four

Harry had loved his walk to the park. The only bad thing about it was returning to the shelter. He wished that Grace hadn't brought him back here. He wasn't sure where she went in-between her visits, but it would be so much nicer if she could take him there with her. She seemed to be sad when they said goodbye as well, so why did she have to leave him behind?

He huddled sadly into the corner of his basket, and sighed, wishing that great big dog across the corridor would just be quiet. He wanted to go to sleep.

Still, Harry was a lot more cheerful than he'd been before he met Grace. His eyes were brighter, and he played in his run, instead of being curled up in his basket all day. Everyone admired him now, and Sally was always showing him off to possible owners.

By the next weekend, Grace was starting to get quite worried. The other volunteers kept telling her how much people admired him, and she could see that when she was there, too.

"It's lucky that Jack Russells need so much exercise," Grace whispered to Harry, as an elderly lady regretfully went on to look for a less energetic dog. "She really liked you. She'd have taken you if Sally hadn't pointed that out. Oh, I don't believe it, Harry, look. More people!"

A family with a boy a little younger than her and a baby girl was looking excitedly at Harry.

"I like this one, Dad!" the boy was saying. "He's a great dog."

The dad looked at Harry frisking round Grace, and smiled. "He does look nice. Do you work here?" he asked Grace.

Grace nodded. "I volunteer after

181

school and at the weekends."

"We're looking for a family dog," the mum put in. "Do you think that" – she looked at his name card – "Harry would be suitable?"

Grace gulped. She looked round quickly to check that none of the staff were close enough to hear, then said quietly, "Um, I'm not sure. Jack Russells aren't great with very young children. They can be a bit snappy if children bother them too much…"

It was actually true, Jack Russells could be snappy. But Harry had never shown signs of anything like that, and Grace knew she was being mean by trying to put them off. She just couldn't bear to see him go to someone else.

"You might want a gentler dog, with your baby," she added. "Have you seen Maggie? She's a cross-breed, but she's really sweet, and so friendly and well-behaved."

Luckily, the family thought Maggie

was lovely, and when Grace left the shelter they were talking with Sally about adopting her. But Grace felt terrible all the way home.

"What's up?" Danny asked her. He'd been exercising Bella and Frisky, a retriever, in the outdoor yard. "You haven't told me anything about all the cute stuff Harry did today. Have you managed to get him to shake hands yet? You reckoned he'd nearly got it."

Grace gave a sad little shrug. "He can almost do it. Danny, one of the families who came today really liked him. I sort of put them off, because they had a baby and Jack Russells aren't good with little kids, but it was mostly because I didn't want them to take him... I don't want him to go," she explained.

"Oh, Gracie," Danny said, putting an arm round her shoulders. "Sally and Mandy warned us when we started. You promised you wouldn't fall in love with any of them."

"I know!" Grace wailed. "But Harry's so gorgeous, Danny, I don't want anyone else to have him except for me!"

Danny sighed. "Well, you managed to put those people off today, but Gracie, you can't be there every time someone likes him. It's going to happen, you know, sooner or later."

"Some help you are," Grace sniffled, but she knew it was true.

It was about to happen even sooner than Grace had thought. Mrs Jameson, the young woman who'd asked Sally about Harry, came back that Sunday. She was a perfect owner. No small children, a big garden for him to play in, and she worked from home some of the time so he wouldn't be too lonely. The shelter staff were delighted.

So was Harry. He'd seen Grace come in just after the lady once before and he assumed they belonged together. So when he saw Sally loading all his toys into his basket, and bringing out his lead for this lady, he was certain that she must be taking him to see Grace. He didn't understand why Grace wasn't fetching him, but he was quite sure that that was where they were going.

"What do you think of your new home, Harry?" As Mrs Jameson put his basket down in the kitchen, Harry looked round with interest. It was nice. Lots of space, and loads of things to sniff and explore. He wondered where Grace was. He sniffed behind all the cupboards, then checked under the table, in case she was hiding. Hopefully she would come soon.

Grace hadn't been able to go to the shelter for a few days – they'd been busy flat-hunting and today was Tuesday, so she had to go to ballet after school.

She crept into the changing room. Luckily, Mum had dropped her off a bit late, so Maya would probably be already changed and in the ballet studio, and Grace wouldn't have to talk to her before the class started. She just knew that Maya was going to ask about Harry, and she still hadn't worked out what to say.

Speedily, Grace changed into her leotard, and put her hair up, then she sneaked into the studio, just in time. She looked round for Maya as they did their warm-up routine, but she couldn't see her. All the way through the class, Grace watched for Maya, but she never arrived.

Grace had got away with it – for one week, anyway.

Grace ran into the shelter on Wednesday afternoon, dashing ahead of Danny. She'd really missed Harry over the last few days; it felt like ages since she'd seen him. And she'd finally finished Harry's toy last night – she couldn't wait to give it to him.

She raced along to Harry's run, and gasped. He'd gone! There was a friendly-looking black spaniel there instead, who woofed an excited hello, and came to greet her. Grace stood by the run, her heart racing, hardly feeling the spaniel licking her fingers.

Maybe he'd been moved? Yes, that was it. Harry must be in one of the other pens, that was all. She said goodbye to the spaniel, who stared after her sadly, and searched the rest of the kennel area. Every pen was full, but none of the dogs was Harry. Sally met her coming in from the outdoor area, her head hanging.

"Oh, Grace! I didn't know you were here yet." Sally looked at her worriedly. "Grace, I'm sorry, I really wanted to tell you before you saw he was gone."

Grace nodded.

"A really nice lady's taken him," Sally promised. "She has a lovely big garden for him to run in."

"Oh," Grace whispered. Then she turned and ran back down the corridor.

Danny was putting a lead on one of the other dogs, a big greyhound that he really liked. He straightened up when Grace brushed past him. "Hey, what's the matter? Grace? Where are you going?" He stared after her, then followed. He had a horrible feeling he already knew what had happened.

Harry lay in his basket, staring sadly round the kitchen. He'd been at his new home for two days now, and his new owners had both had to go to work today. He was all alone. He hadn't liked the noise and bustle of the shelter, but it felt very strange for things to be so quiet.

And where was Grace? He had been sure that this was her house and he was going to live with her, but it had been ages and she still hadn't come. He was beginning to have a horrible feeling that the wrong person had brought him home, and he didn't know what to do about it.

At least it wasn't dark now. The

kitchen was very frightening at night, and he howled for someone to come and keep him company. At Beth's house he had been allowed to sleep on her bed, never shut up on his own all night.

Mrs Jameson had come downstairs and comforted him the first night, but she wasn't the person he really wanted. Mr Jameson patted him occasionally, but he kept sniffing, and he sneezed whenever Harry came close to him. His sneezes were very loud, and quite scary. Harry was spending an awful lot of time shut up on his own in the kitchen, because he and Mr Jameson didn't seem to be able to be in the same room together.

Harry sighed. Maybe someone would come and play with him soon.

Maybe even Grace. He really hoped so.
But Beth had gone, and not come back.
Had Grace left him now, too?

Chapter Five

Danny went to the shelter on his own on Thursday. He tried to get Grace to come with him, but she wouldn't. When he got back, he went to her room and tried to cheer her up with funny stories about Finn, his current favourite at the shelter. Finn was half Labrador, half no-one-knew-what, except that it was very big and very hungry. Danny had had to own up to Sally that Finn had found half a packet of mints in his pocket, and wolfed them down before Danny could stop him. But luckily, Sally had come to look at Finn, and said she thought it would probably take about six packets of mints to do anything to him; he had an iron stomach.

The story only earned Danny a very small smile. But on Friday after school, he set to work again. "You know, it's not fair on Sally and all the other dogs if you don't go," he pointed out.

"What do you mean?" Grace asked worriedly. She liked Sally a lot; she really didn't want to upset her.

"Well, she's used to having you there to help. If we don't go, the dogs won't get as many walks. I'm taking Finn out again today, but what about Bella and Jake and Harrison? I can't walk all of them, Grace, and not many other people come in to help during the week."

Grace nodded. He was right. It was just hard to imagine going back to the shelter and Harry not being there.

"And don't forget how good everyone at the shelter said you were with the dogs. It'd be a real shame if you stopped going." Danny looked at her hopefully. "Shall I phone Mum, and tell her I'm not dropping you at home, you're coming with me?" He whipped his mobile out of his pocket.

Grace sighed. "I suppose so."

"Excellent!" Danny cheered.

Sally said that Jake could really do with a walk, and that Grace and Danny could take him and Finn to the park together.

Grace tried not to be too miserable – it wasn't fair on Jake for a start; he was a lovely dog, a Westie with a beautiful white coat. It was hard though. She couldn't help remembering the brilliant walk she'd had with Harry.

Finn dragged Danny off to bark at squirrels in the trees on one side of the park, and Grace wandered slowly round the play area with Jake. He was an elderly dog, whose previous owner had died, and he liked gentle walks.

"Grace! Hello!" Someone was calling from the swings, and Grace looked over and saw Maya. Grace smiled and waved at her, but then her smile faded. How was she going to explain Jake?

"Did you miss me at ballet last week?" Maya called, slipping off the swing and running over. "I had a tummy bug, and Mum said if I was missing school, I couldn't go to ballet." Maya looked down at Jake, and then up again, confused. "That's not the same dog you had last time, is it? The other one had a pointier nose, and – and stuff."

"Um, yes…" Grace muttered.

"Wow, have you got two dogs now?" Maya asked excitedly.

Grace stared down at Jake and shook her head. She was too embarrassed to look at Maya. "I haven't got a dog, they aren't mine. Neither of them." Then she pulled on Jake's lead and suddenly dragged him off across the park.

Maya stood staring after them, looking surprised and rather upset.

Grace found Danny trying to persuade Finn to leave the squirrels alone, and told him what had happened. She was almost crying.

"So you just ran off?" Danny asked disbelievingly.

"Yes…" Grace admitted.

"You muppet. Why didn't you explain? I bet she would've understood."

"No, she wouldn't. I'd have to admit I lied to her when I met her that time with Harry. I let her think he was mine, Danny. I never actually said it, but I didn't tell her no when she said he was."

Danny blinked as he worked that one out. "I still think she'd understand if you explained it properly. You'll have to anyway. She's bound to ask you at ballet. Or else she'll be really off with you, and you'll be all miserable every Tuesday."

"I could stop going to ballet…" Grace suggested desperately.

"Like Mum's going to let you do that, silly! How can you be so good at getting dogs to understand you, but too shy to talk to people properly?" Danny shook his head. "Nope, you'll just have to explain. Is she still here?"

They looked over at the play area. Maya was there, talking to her sister.

"Come on!" And Danny grabbed Grace's arms and marched her and Finn and Jake across the park.

Grace slowly approached Maya, looking embarrassed.

"Go on!" Danny nudged her.

"I'm so sorry," Grace muttered. "I didn't mean to pretend Harry was mine, but when you thought he was, it was so nice. I really, really wanted him to belong to me, you see."

Maya gave her a confused look, confused and slightly suspicious. "So neither of them are yours? Who do they belong to then?"

Grace sighed sadly. "The animal shelter. Me and Danny go and help there after school. We take the dogs for walks."

"Ohhh." Maya nodded.

"I didn't mean to run off, it's just that I suddenly realized you'd know I'd lied to you and I didn't know how to explain everything." Grace looked at Maya, hopefully. Danny had been so sure that if she explained, Maya would be OK with it. Was he right?

"If you liked Harry so much, why didn't you take him home?" Maya asked.

"Mum says we can't fit a dog in our flat." Grace sighed. "But Harry was so sad when he first came to the shelter. I spent ages trying to cheer him up, and it was almost like he was mine. When you thought he actually belonged to me, it was like my wish come true."

"At least you can see him at the shelter," Maya said. "It sounds like fun."

Grace sighed. "I can't any more. Someone else adopted him at the weekend; that's why I've got Jake today instead. Harry's gone."

"Oh, Grace! That's so sad." They were silent for a minute, then Maya looked at her and Danny shyly. "So you still go to the shelter? Could I maybe come with you one day? I love dogs too; I'd really like to see them all."

"Oh, yes! Why don't you meet us there tomorrow?" Grace smiled. "Mum said we could definitely go on Saturday morning, didn't she, Danny? And they're always wanting more help."

Grace never even noticed that someone else was there in the park. Mrs Jameson was working from home, and had taken Harry out for a quick walk. He was enjoying the smells – the park was full of interesting litter bins, and squirrels, and the scents of other dogs – but he wished he was with Grace. He plodded slowly round the path, watching the other dogs, and the children playing. He wondered where Grace was now.

And then he saw her. Grace was over on the other side of the park – with another dog. Harry stopped dead, and ignored Mrs Jameson gently pulling at his lead. Had she forgotten him already? Harry barked and barked, pulling on his lead as hard as he could,

but she was too far away to hear him. Did Grace have another dog now? He missed her so much, as much as he'd missed Beth when she went away. Why did everyone go away? Harry sat down in the middle of the path and howled broken-heartedly.

Mrs Jameson was worried that he might be hurt somehow. She picked him up and hurried him home, where he curled up in his basket and wouldn't be played with all evening. He even refused to eat. He felt so lonely and he wanted Grace to come back for him so much. Why did she have another dog now? Didn't she love him any more?

Mrs Jameson just didn't know what was wrong with Harry and when her husband got home from work she told him how upset Harry seemed. "I want him to be happy here, but he doesn't seem to be settling in at all," she admitted.

Mr Jameson sighed. "I'm not sure this is working out either…"

Mrs Jameson nodded sadly. "I know.

We can't just keep shutting Harry in the kitchen, and your allergy's getting worse every day."

Mr Jameson gave her a hug. "I'm sorry, I know you really wanted a dog..."

His wife smiled. "But it isn't fair on either of you. I'll ring the shelter and arrange to take him back there tomorrow." She sniffed. "Poor little Harry..."

Chapter Six

Maya and her sister were waiting outside for Grace when she and Danny and Mum arrived on Saturday afternoon. Maya was going to stay for a couple of hours and then her sister was coming back to pick her up. Grace was delighted to have someone to show round, and Maya loved meeting all the dogs. They were just saying hello to

Jake, the Westie, when Grace heard a familiar yap from the next pen. She turned slowly to look. Could it be…

"Harry!" Grace cried, and he bounded up to the door of the pen, leaping and barking delightedly.

"Oh, it's really you, what are you doing back here, you lovely boy?" Grace murmured, stroking him through the wire.

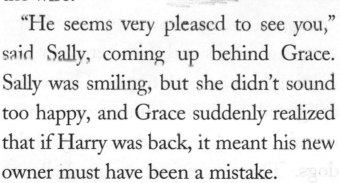

"He seems very pleased to see you," said Sally, coming up behind Grace. Sally was smiling, but she didn't sound too happy, and Grace suddenly realized that if Harry was back, it meant his new owner must have been a mistake.

"Did the people not want him after all?" she asked, gazing fondly at Harry.

Sally sighed. "Harry didn't settle very well, unfortunately. I'm sure he would have been fine, given time, but the husband turned out to be allergic to dogs, too. Poor Harry, back here again, aren't you, sweetheart?"

Grace looked at Harry lovingly. She slipped into his run, and sat down, letting him climb all over her, and lick as much of her as he could. She was so glad to see him again. But then a horrible thought struck her. Harry hadn't settled at his new home – was that her fault? Because she'd been spending so much time with him? If he was too fond of her, he might not want to go to a new owner.

"What's the matter?" Maya asked. "Aren't you pleased he's back?"

Grace sighed. "I am pleased. But Sally said he didn't settle at his new home. What if that's because he's spending too much time with me?"

Maya looked confused, and Grace tried to explain. "He's going to be rehomed again – what if I spoil another new home for him, too? Maybe I just shouldn't see him any more."

Harry lay blissfully in Grace's lap, his paws folded on his stomach, eyes closed. The only thing that could make this better would be some food. He was fairly sure dinner would be here soon...

"Harry... Harry..." Grace was whispering to him. "I've got to go, sweetie. It's time for you to be fed." She lifted him gently off her lap.

Harry slid sleepily off, and looked up at her, puzzled. She was going? Again? But she'd only just come back! Grace was opening the door of his pen, and he flung himself at her, howling. No! He didn't want her to go, she might not come again!

Grace shut the door of the run, her fingers trembling. Harry was howling so loudly, everyone in the shelter was looking round, wondering what was happening.

Sally walked quickly towards them. "Don't worry, Grace, I've got some food for him; hopefully that'll help calm him down. You go. See you soon, OK? Don't worry about Harry, he's just had a hard couple of days."

Grace nodded, blinking back tears. It was really hard to leave him when he was so upset. Maya and Danny were hurrying up the corridor towards her, looking worried.

"Maya told me Harry was back. Was that him howling?" Danny asked.

Grace nodded and sniffed. Danny gave her a hug and they headed for the door. Mum was waving to them from reception, telling them to hurry up.

Maya had just opened the door when there was a sudden crash, and they turned back to see that Sally had dropped Harry's food bowl. It looked like he'd jumped at the door of the pen as she'd opened it, and knocked into her. Now he was racing down between the pens, barking madly, with Sally chasing after him.

Harry settled at Grace's feet, his tail wagging desperately. Other people were allowed to take him home. Why couldn't she? She was the one he wanted to go home with!

Hopefully, he held out one paw, the way she'd been teaching him. Grace's eyes were full of tears as she crouched down to take it. Harry gave a triumphant little bark. He'd done it right. There. Surely she couldn't send him back to his run now.

Grace picked him up, and rubbed her cheek against his smooth fur. Then she handed him back to Sally, and ran.

She couldn't bear to see him like this.

Danny, Maya and Mum found her outside the shelter, leaning against the wall and crying.

"Oh, Grace…" Mum said worriedly. "I'm sure he'll be all right in a minute." Grace gave her a disbelieving look, and Mum sighed. "Well, maybe not straight away, but I'm sure he will get over it."

"But it isn't fair!" Grace sobbed. "He's always having to get over things. His first owner had to leave him, and now this one's given up on him, and he just wants to be with me and I can't have him!"

Mum put an arm round her shoulders comfortingly, and Danny asked, "Mum, isn't there any way we could have him? You know how hard Grace has worked."

"I do know, and I'm really proud of you, Grace. But Harry needs lots of space to run around. And he'd hate being shut up while we're all out during the day. I'm sorry, Grace, I wish things were different, but you know we can't have a dog at the moment."

Chapter Seven

"He's as bad as he was when he first came," Mandy said sadly, looking at the little brown-and-white ball in the basket. It was all they'd been able to see of Harry for days.

Sally called gently, "Harry! Here, boy!" but he didn't even twitch. "It's so sad. He really adored Grace, but I can understand why she doesn't think she should visit him any more, and it's probably for the best."

"Still, there's a family coming to see him this afternoon," said Mandy. "They saw him on the website, and they think he looks perfect. If they like him, and they can give him the time to settle down…"

They stared at Harry, still curled up silently, and Sally sighed. "Well, you never know…"

Grace didn't go to the shelter at all that week. She just couldn't bear it. She had made Harry's life even harder by falling in love with him. He had to find a new home, and she was stopping him.

She just had to let him go, the sooner the better.

She supposed she could have gone back to the shelter and kept away from Harry, but that would be so difficult. Danny didn't even try to persuade her this time. Mum had phoned the shelter to talk to Sally and explain. Grace had listened to what Mum was saying, and she could tell that Sally was sad, but that she agreed with Mum. It was the best thing for Harry.

Life felt very flat without the shelter to go to, though, Grace thought, lying on her bed listening to her favourite CD. School, more school, hanging around at home. She'd gone to Maya's for tea yesterday, which was nice, but she still missed Harry, and all the other dogs, so much.

"Grace!" Mum called from the kitchen. "Time to go!"

Grace sighed, and rolled off her bed. Another flat to go and see.

Grace smiled politely as the lady who owned the flat chatted to her about whether she liked the bedroom that would be hers. She just wished Mum and Dad would stop fussing about the bathroom and get on, she was so sick of flat-hunting. They'd already seen this flat anyway, yesterday, when Grace and Danny were at school. Why did they need to look at everything again?

They finished at last, and Sheila, the owner, led them back towards the kitchen. "I'll just show you the garden," she said over her shoulder. "I've had a bit of a tidy-up since you saw it yesterday, but I'm afraid I'm not much of a gardener."

Grace gasped. "A garden! There's a garden?"

Sheila turned back and smiled. "Yes, didn't your parents say? The garden goes with this ground-floor flat, you see."

Grace looked at Mum and Dad, her eyes wide with hope. "So could we...?"

Mum nodded and laughed. "Yes! I mean, it'll take a little while before we can move in, of course. But your dad and I have talked this over and, yes, we can have Harry."

Grace flung herself at her mum and hugged her. "You planned all this, I can't believe it!"

Her mum laughed and led her over to the window. "When we saw it, we realized how perfect it would be for you and Danny. You've both worked so hard at the shelter. Now you get to have your own dog."

They looked out at the garden. It was messy, full of weeds, but Grace could just imagine Harry bounding up and down, barking joyfully as she threw a ball for him to chase.

Danny stared out too, his face split by an enormous grin, but then he frowned. "What about us all being out in the daytime? You said we couldn't leave Harry alone all day."

Dad nodded. "It's OK. I've spoken to the people at work, and they're happy for me to take Harry into the office with me some of the time. And when I have a heavy day of meetings, your mum should be able to pop home and give him a walk in her lunch hour."

"Oh, Dad!" Grace hugged him, and then her mum again. "Thank you so much! Can we go home and ring the shelter now?"

When they got back, Grace was standing hopefully holding the phone before anyone else had even got their coat off. She'd even found the number on the kitchen noticeboard.

"All right, all right!" Mum laughed and took the phone.

Grace waited with her fingernails digging into her palms, listening to the ringing at the other end.

"Oh, hello, could I speak to Sally, please? Oh, it is you, hi, Sally. This is Amanda Winter, Grace and Danny's mum. Yes, we're all fine, thank you, we've missed you, too. But actually, we've got some good news. We're moving, and we're going to have more space in our new flat. We think we might be able to adopt Harry after all." Mum smiled excitedly at Grace, but then there was a long pause, and the smile faded. Her voice had flattened when she next spoke. "Oh. Oh, I see. Yes, well, that's good. Yes. We should have expected it. I'll tell her. Thanks. Bye."

"Someone else has taken him, haven't they?" Grace asked, her voice shaking, and Mum nodded.

"Oh, Gracie, I'm so sorry." She sighed. "Sally said he's gone to a family this time. The children aren't too young for a dog, and they're all keen on having him. He'll be having a lovely time..." But she couldn't make the words sound happy.

"If only we'd found the flat sooner," Grace wailed.

"It's terrible luck," Mum agreed. "We'll just have to try and be happy for Harry. I know it's hard."

Dad picked up Grace and hugged her, even though he was always saying she was too big for him to do that now. Danny sat at the kitchen table with his chin on his hands, staring out of the window. "I can't believe we just missed him," he muttered. "It isn't fair..."

"You probably don't want to think about this right now," Dad said slowly. "But – there are other dogs. Loads of dogs at the shelter who need a home."

"Not yet," Grace interrupted. "We couldn't just yet."

"No, I know. But think about it. Harry's found a lovely home. But we could give a home to another dog."

Grace nodded, and sniffed. At last she said slowly, "Maybe. We could have Finn, he's your favourite, isn't he, Danny? The one who ate your mints?" Her voice was shaking.

Danny nodded. "But I think he's too big, even for a flat with a garden. Harry would have been perfect..."

"He would, wouldn't he?" Grace tried to smile. "I suppose at least now I can go and help at the shelter again, without worrying about upsetting Harry. Oh, I do hope he likes the new people! He deserves a better chance this time!"

Chapter Eight

It was just over a week later, and Grace was sitting in her new bedroom. It was much bigger than her old one, but she hadn't finished unpacking her things yet. She just couldn't summon up the energy. Mum kept telling her to get on, but Grace couldn't help stopping to look out of her window, imagining Harry playing out there. If she half-closed her eyes, she could almost see him, hiding under that big bush, getting ready to leap out at her...

Grace rubbed her hand across her eyes. Harry had a new home now. It was a lovely family Sally had said, when she went back to help at the shelter. He would be over the moon, with so many people to love him. The

 tears started to run down her cheeks again as she pictured him, curled up on a bed just like this one, while a girl the same age as her stroked him gently.

Harry was pulling anxiously at his lead as Sam Ashcroft coaxed him to chase the ball. The children were so bouncy and excited, and it was just too much for him. Harry had had such a hard time recently – moving around all over the place, and having to get used to so many new people. He simply wasn't ready for three energetic children who wanted him to play all the time.

"Why won't he chase it?" Sam asked crossly. "I've been trying for ages."

"Maybe he's tired?" Luke suggested. "Mum's over there chatting to that lady from school, we'd better tell her."

"But I don't want to go home!" Lily wailed, and Harry flinched at the noise.

Mrs Ashcroft said goodbye to her friend and walked over to the children. "Come on, guys, we need to get home. Sally from the shelter's coming to see how we're doing with Harry."

Harry plodded along the pavement with Luke, jumping when cars whooshed past. Everything seemed frightening at the moment. He wished he could just curl up in his basket, and everyone would leave him alone. His ears were tensely pricked for the whole walk, and when a piece of litter blew in front of him, he gave a sharp, frightened little bark.

Mrs Ashcroft looked at him worriedly, but she didn't say anything.

The children were even noisier than usual when they got home. After Lily had nearly run him over twice with her doll's pram, Harry decided to take drastic action. He hid under the sofa. It was quiet, it was dark, and nobody could find him to make him chase balls, or jump into boxes, or even just to hug him. He didn't want to be hugged right now.

The doorbell rang, and Harry shuddered as the children thundered down the hallway to the door.

"I just don't know where he could've got to," Mrs Ashcroft was saying worriedly. "We came back from our walk about twenty minutes ago. He must have slipped away somewhere."

"Is he settling in well?" It was a familiar voice. Harry was sure he knew it. It wasn't Grace, but it made him think of her. He poked his nose out from under the sofa so as to hear better.

"There he is!" Lily shrieked, and Harry promptly shot back underneath.

Lily crouched down to peer under the sofa, and Harry backed away from her. She swept her hand underneath, and called to him to come out. Harry barked anxiously. Why wouldn't they just leave him alone?

"Lily, stop that!" Mrs Ashcroft said worriedly. "Now, Lily!"

Harry was still barking, a sharp, unhappy bark that sounded like a warning. *Leave me alone! Go away!*

Lily scrambled up, her bottom lip wobbling. "I don't like it when he barks like that," she said tearfully.

Mrs Ashcroft sighed, and looked at Sally. "I was hoping to be able to tell you he was starting to settle in," she said. "But I just don't think he is. The children have tried really hard, but I think we're a bit too much for him to take. He's a lovely little dog, but he just doesn't seem very happy."

Sally nodded sadly. "I think you're right. I've got a dog-carrier in my car. I'm so sorry it hasn't worked out.

Hopefully we can find you another dog, one that's used to a busy house."

Mrs Ashcroft and the children left Sally to coax Harry out, which she managed by being very quiet, and opening a packet of dog treats.

Then it was back to the animal shelter – again.

"He really is the boomerang dog, isn't he?" Sally sighed, as she and Mandy watched Harry eating his breakfast on Sunday morning.

"It's such a pity Grace couldn't take him home," Mandy said. "She built up such a fantastic relationship with him."

Sally nodded, then she smiled slowly.

"Of course! You've given me a brilliant idea! I wonder if Grace and Danny are coming in today? I might give their mum and dad a call."

She came back out of reception smiling. "They'll be here shortly. I can't wait to see Grace's reaction."

Mandy was frowning. "But I thought you'd decided that Harry loving Grace so much was stopping him settling with a new owner? Are you sure you want him to see her again?"

Sally nodded. "But I didn't tell you – the family's moved. They wanted to adopt Harry, but he'd already gone to the Ashcrofts. They were going to think about another dog when they felt ready. And I've told them that the perfect dog has just arrived..."

Grace pushed open the door to the dogs' area, leading the way for Mum and Dad and Danny. Her hands felt sweaty, and slipped on the door handle. She was so nervous. Sally had said that a wonderful new dog had arrived, one who would be perfect for Grace and her family.

Why wasn't she happy?

All she could think of was Harry. She tried desperately to picture him with those other children, having a brilliant time. This other dog really needed a home, too.

"You all right?" Danny asked her, looking at her thoughtfully.

"I suppose," Grace whispered. "It just feels odd."

"I know." He sighed. "But this dog will be fab, too."

Grace grabbed his arm. "Look!"

Sally was walking down the passage, carrying a puppy in her arms. A Jack Russell puppy, white with brown patches, whose ears pricked up as he heard Grace's voice. He gave one joyful bark, and twisted right out of Sally's hold, leaping to the ground, his paws scrabbling frantically as he raced towards them.

"Harry! It's Harry!" Grace scooped him up, and he licked her face delightedly, all over, then generously leaned out of her arms to lick Danny, too. He'd missed Grace so much, and she'd come, she'd come back for him!

Sally grinned. "Told you I had the perfect dog…"

"I can't believe it," Grace whispered, hugging Harry tightly. "Thank you so much!" she told Sally.

Sally smiled at her. "I'm just glad he's found the right home at last. I don't think he'll be coming back to us again. But you have to do me one favour. Will you write to Beth, his old owner, for me? Tell her all about Harry's new home?"

"Of course!" Grace nodded eagerly.

Harry looked round to see Sally fetching his basket and toys out of the run, and handing them to Danny. She gave Grace his lead. Harry's stubby little tail wagged delightedly as Grace clipped it on. He'd never seen Grace look this happy before. He gave her a hopeful look. If his basket and his toys were coming…

Grace was staring at him with shining eyes. "Oh, Harry! You're really coming home with us. We don't have to say goodbye this time."

"Harry, don't chew that pencil," Grace giggled. "Dogs aren't meant to eat pencils. It's not good for you."

She reached over to her bedside table. "Look, have a biscuit bone instead. But don't leave any crumbs on the duvet, OK? Mum's not sure about you being on my bed; we don't want to give her anything to complain about!"

Harry gnawed happily on the dog biscuit, letting Grace chat away. He loved it when she talked to him. Perhaps after she'd finished this thing she was doing they could go to the park, with Danny too. He gulped the last of the bone, and stretched out his paws. She was still writing. He'd have a little sleep.

Grace looked down at him lovingly, curled up next to her teddy. She couldn't believe Harry had found a home at last – with her.

Dear Beth,

Sally gave me your address so I could write and tell you all about Harry. He has been living with us for two weeks now, and he is lovely. (I know you know this already!) I really hope you're enjoying living in New York, and you don't miss him too much.

Did Harry like smoky bacon crisps when he lived with you? He stole a whole packet out of my brother's bag yesterday. Luckily Danny loves him so much he went and got him another packet from the newsagent's. Mum was really cross, but it's OK, Harry wasn't sick.

Harry loves playing in our garden and going for walks, and he's very clever at doing tricks now. He can shake hands, and roll over, and he'll almost stay, but not if you put a dog biscuit in front of him, we're still working on that one!

Lots of love,
Grace and Harry

Buttons the Runaway Puppy

For Phoebe

Chapter One

"Wait for me!" Sophie called after her twin brothers. She was pedalling as fast as she could, but they were so much bigger than she was, and they'd had enormous new mountain bikes for their birthday last month. There was no way she could catch them up if they didn't slow down a bit. "Tom! Michael! Wait for me! Please!"

Tom and Michael circled round and hurtled back towards her, braking and pulling up in a cloud of dust.

"Come on, Sophie! You must be able to pedal a *bit* faster," Michael told her, laughing.

"Aw, now that's not fair, Mikey, she's only got little legs." Tom grinned at Sophie, and she scowled back.

"Can't we have a rest for a minute anyway?" she begged. "I want to watch the dogs, and this is the best bit of the common for that. I want to see if any of the ones I know are out for walks today."

"Yeah, I don't mind," Tom agreed.

Michael rolled his eyes. "Just for a minute. You're dog-mad, Sophie Martin!" he told her, grinning.

They wheeled their bikes out of the way of the path, and then slumped on a bench. All three of them stared out across the common, which was packed with dogs and their owners. This was definitely the best place for dog-watching: raised up on a little hill, they could see all the way around.

"Look, Sophie, there's that mad Red Setter you like." Michael pointed at a dog frisking about on one of the paths, its dark reddish coat gleaming in the sunlight.

Sophie giggled as she watched him running round and round in circles, and worrying at sticks. His owner was trying to get him to fetch a ball, but the big dog was having none of it.

Tom sighed. "If I had a dog, I'd train

it an awful lot better than that one. Poor thing doesn't know whether it's coming or going."

"I don't think it's very easy to train a dog," Sophie said.

"Of course it isn't," Tom agreed. "That's why there's so many badly behaved dogs around. People can't be bothered to train their dogs properly, and they just let them do whatever they want because it's easier than getting them to behave."

"OK then, if you could have any dog you want, what would you have?" Michael asked. "Mum and Dad keep saying that one day we can. Dad didn't say 'no' straight away last time I asked."

Tom whistled through his teeth. "Nothing small and yappy. A dog you could take on proper walks. Maybe a Dalmatian."

"Mmm, I could go for a Dalmatian. Or a Golden Retriever," Michael mused. "Wouldn't it be great to get a dog now, just before the summer holidays? We'd have all summer to go for really long walks."

Tom nodded. "Don't get your hopes up. What would you have, Sophie?"

Sophie was staring back down the path that they'd come up. "I'd have a Labrador. But a chocolate one, like Buttons. I *think* that's her coming up the path now. Oh dear..."

"What's she done this time?" Tom asked.

Sophie put her hand over her mouth to stifle her giggles, as the chocolate-brown Labrador puppy danced around her owner, tangling him in her lead.

"Whoops," Tom muttered, and Michael bobbed up from the bench to see what was going on.

"Ow, that must've hurt. Do you think we should go and help?"

Buttons was standing on the path, looking down at her owner in confusion.

What on earth are you doing down there? she seemed to be saying. Her owner unwrapped her lead from his ankles grimly, and started to heave himself up out of the bramble bush.

Sophie looked at Tom and Michael. "We probably should, but Buttons's owner is so grumpy, he might shout at us."

"He's called Mr Jenkins," Tom told her. "I heard one of his neighbours talking to him when we walked past his house the other day."

Michael nodded. "I think Sophie's right, he's probably hoping no one saw. We'd better be looking the other way when he comes past."

All three children stared innocently over the common towards the lake, pretending not to have seen Buttons trip up Mr Jenkins.

"Good morning!" Michael called politely, as the old man walked by, trying to hold Buttons back to heel. Mr Jenkins lived on the next road across from the Martins, with his garden backing on to theirs, so they saw him quite often. Their mum always said hello when she passed him.

"Hmmph," Mr Jenkins grunted, and stomped on past.

"You see! So grumpy!" Sophie whispered, as he disappeared down the path.

"Yes, but I'd be grumpy too, if I'd just fallen in a bramble bush," Tom pointed out.

Buttons appreciated them saying hello, anyway. She looked back and barked in a friendly way as Mr Jenkins hurried her along. She liked those children. They always smiled when they saw her, and the girl had once asked politely to stroke her. Mr Jenkins had let her, and she'd said how beautiful Buttons was and scratched behind her ears as well.

"Come on, Buttons," Mr Jenkins grumbled, and Buttons sighed. He was cross with her again. She hadn't *meant* to trip him up. There were so many good smells on the common, and she couldn't help it if they were on different sides of the path. She'd had to go and investigate them all, and the silly lead had got itself tangled in his legs. It just showed that leads were not a good idea. She much preferred to run along without one. Especially if there were squirrels.

They were coming to the part of the common with the trees now, and there was bound to be a squirrel. Buttons looked up and barked hopefully.

"No, I'm not letting you off your

lead, silly dog," Mr Jenkins told her, but he patted her lovingly on the head at the same time, and she knew he wasn't cross any more. "No, because you'll be in the next county before I catch up with you. I'm sorry, Buttons girl, we need to head home. My legs aren't what they used to be, especially when I've been dragged through a bramble bush. Come on, home now."

Buttons whined sadly. She understood some words, and *home* was one of them. Not home already? It felt like it hadn't been a very long walk at all. She wanted lots of walks – in fact a whole day of walks, with a few quick sleeps and a couple of big meals in between, would be perfect.

"Look, Mum, Buttons is in her garden again." Sophie nudged her mother's arm as they walked past Mr Jenkins's house. The summer holidays had started, and it was so hot that they were going to cool off at the pool. "She keeps scrabbling at the fence like she wants to get out. She was doing that yesterday, when I went past on my way to say goodbye to Rachel. I heard her barking loads when I was out in the garden, too."

Mum stopped and looked thoughtfully over the fence at Buttons. "Have you seen Mr Jenkins about recently?" she asked Sophie. "I haven't for a while, and I do usually meet him in the shops every so often."

Sophie shook her head. "Not since that day in the park a couple of weeks ago, when Buttons tripped him up. I definitely haven't seen him since school finished, and that's a whole week."

She sighed. Only one week of the summer holidays gone. She ought to be looking forward to another five weeks off school, but yesterday her best friend Rachel had gone off to Ireland to stay with her family for the whole holiday. Sophie couldn't imagine what she was going to do all summer, without Rachel's house to hang out at. She was sick of Michael and Tom already. Not only were they her big brothers, so they thought they could always boss her around, but they were each other's best friends. They didn't want their little sister tagging along the whole time. She and Rachel had promised to keep in touch by email and send each other lots of fun postcards and things. But it wasn't the same as having your best friend living just round the corner.

Buttons looked up at Sophie and barked hopefully. *Walk? Please?* she begged. She recognized Sophie, who often spoke to her when she went past. Buttons could sometimes hear her in the garden, too. Sophie had a sweet voice and always sounded friendly.

"Poor Buttons, she looks really sad," Sophie said, wishing she could stroke her. She knew Buttons was friendly, but Mum had made her promise not to stroke dogs without asking the owner first.

"Thinking about it, I did see Mr Jenkins in the supermarket last week, and he was walking with a stick," Mum said slowly. "I wonder if he hasn't been able to take Buttons for walks, and that's why she's scratching like that. She wants to get out."

"Sorry, Buttons, we're going swimming, or else we'd love to take you for a walk. Oh, look, I'm sure she knows what we're saying, her ears just drooped, and she isn't wagging her tail any more," Sophie said as she waved goodbye.

Buttons stared after them with big, sad brown eyes. She hadn't been on a proper walk in a long time. Mr Jenkins was very good about letting her in and out of the house whenever she wanted, but he just didn't seem to want to walk her right now. The garden was quite big – it went all round the house from front to back – but it wasn't the same as walks. Buttons whined sadly, and scratched at the fence again. She thought she might be able to go for a walk by herself, if she could only get over this fence. Or under it, perhaps.

"Buttons! Buttons!" She could hear Mr Jenkins calling, and her ears pricked up immediately. Maybe he was feeling better, and he wanted to go for a walk after all. She shot round to the back door, which Mr Jenkins was holding open for her.

"There you are! You've been out a while, Buttons." Mr Jenkins stooped down to pat her, holding tight to his stick.

Buttons looked up at him hopefully, and then looked over at her lead, which was hanging on a hook above Mr Jenkins's wellies. She gave an excited little bark, and wagged her tail so fast it blurred.

"Oh, Buttons, I wish we could. I wish we could, poor little girl. Soon, I promise."

Buttons's tail sagged, and she trailed slowly into the living room to curl up on her cushion next to Mr Jenkins's chair. He sat down beside her, and stroked her head lovingly. Buttons licked his hand. She adored Mr Jenkins, even though he couldn't always take her for walks.

Chapter Two

"If you're going along the canal path, you have to be really careful," Mum warned them. "Especially you, Sophie. No going close to the edge, promise?"

"I'm not a baby, Mum! I'm sensible!" Sophie complained. "OK, I promise to be careful."

"All right then. Tom and Michael, you'll keep an eye on her, won't you?

Don't leave her behind."

Sophie's older brothers nodded, eager to get out on their ride, even if it did mean taking Sophie, too.

It was a gorgeous, sunny Saturday afternoon, and Mum and Dad were repainting the kitchen, so it was definitely a good time to be out of the house. The canal path was the Martin family's other favourite place to go on walks and bike rides. They were lucky that it wasn't far from where they lived.

Despite what they'd said to Mum, Michael and Tom couldn't resist speeding off ahead. Every so often one of them would double back to check Sophie was OK, and she was – she quite liked riding along on her own anyway. It meant she could stop and talk to the ginger cat sitting on the fence – he let her stroke him today – and admire the butterflies on a lilac tree that grew on the corner just as she came out on to the canal bank. She could do all these things without the boys telling her to hurry up all the time.

Sophie pedalled along, keeping away from the edge like Mum had told her to. The canal was beautiful, especially with the sun sparkling on it like it was today, but beneath the glitter the water was deep and dark. She rounded the bend, expecting to see Tom and Michael coming back to check on her, but instead she saw a familiar-looking dog.

Buttons!

The pretty little Labrador was sniffing about at the water's edge. Sophie cycled closer, smiling at Buttons's big chocolate paws, and her floppy puppy ears.

Sophie looked around for Mr Jenkins, but she couldn't see him anywhere, and she had a horrible feeling that Buttons had run off. She wasn't old enough or sensible enough to be off the lead – and she wasn't, it was trailing in the mud. Buttons must've pulled it out of Mr Jenkins's hand.

Buttons hadn't noticed Sophie. She was watching a stick that was floating down the canal, and wondering whether she could reach it, if she just leaned over a little. It looked like such a good one — big and long and really muddy — and it was ever so close. She leaned out over the water. If she could just get the end of it in her teeth… But it was still a bit too far away. She tried again, reaching a little further out.

"Buttons! Don't!" Sophie called. "You'll fall!"

Surprised by Sophie's shout, Buttons stepped back quickly. But the edge of the canal bank was muddy and slippery, and her paws skidded. Panicking, she tried to scramble back up the bank, but she was sliding further in, and she couldn't stop herself.

Sophie flung down her bike, and raced to grab Buttons's lead. She caught it just as both of the puppy's front paws slid into the water. Sophie pulled hard on the lead, leaning right back – Buttons might only be little, but she was heavy. Just for a moment, Sophie wondered if Buttons might accidentally pull her into the water, too, but she finally hauled Buttons back on to the bank.

She hugged the shivering puppy tightly. "It's all right, Buttons. Oh dear, your paws are all wet. It's OK, don't worry," Sophie murmured soothingly, trying to calm her down. Buttons buried her nose in Sophie's T-shirt, breathing in her comforting smell. Sophie had saved her!

"Buttons! Buttons!" Mr Jenkins was hurrying up, walking as fast as he could with his stick. "What happened, did she fall in?" he asked worriedly. "I saw you pulling her lead, are you all right? Is she all right?"

He leaned down slowly to stroke Buttons, and she pressed herself against his legs, making frightened little whimpering noises. "Oh, Buttons, you silly girl, what have you been doing?"

He looked up and smiled apologetically at Sophie. "She pulled her lead out of my hand and raced off. It's the first time we've been for a walk in a while. Buttons is a bit overexcited to be out again."

Sophie smiled back at him, though her heart was still thumping. It had been a scary moment. "She didn't go right in. She was just starting to slip, but I grabbed her lead before she did more than get her paws wet."

"Sophie! Are you OK?" Tom and Michael had come riding up, and they looked worried. The little sister they were supposed to be looking after was sitting on the canal bank with a wet dog, her bike flung down on the grass.

"Were you messing about by the

water? Mum told you to stay away from the edge!" Tom shouted.

"Of course I wasn't!" Sophie said indignantly.

Mr Jenkins looked up at the boys. "Your sister stopped Buttons falling in. She's a star. Ooof." He slowly straightened up. "I think we were a bit ambitious with this walk, Buttons. Best leave it a couple of days more."

"Would you like me to walk Buttons home for you?" Sophie asked.

Mr Jenkins smiled at her. "It's very kind of you to offer, but you weren't going home yet, were you? I don't want to take you out of your way."

"That's all right. Isn't it?" Sophie asked Tom and Michael. "Mum wouldn't mind if I went back, would she?"

The boys exchanged glances. "We'll come too," said Tom. "That way we can wheel your bike while you're walking Buttons."

"Oh! I'd forgotten my bike," Sophie admitted. "I was too excited about getting to walk such a gorgeous puppy."

"She is lovely, isn't she?" Mr Jenkins agreed, as they all started to walk home slowly. "Bit of a handful at the moment though. She's got so much energy."

Buttons was darting here and there, sniffing excitedly at the scents of other dogs and people. Sophie laughed as she followed her, but she could see that such a bouncy little dog would be hard work for Mr Jenkins.

"I really need to take her to some dog-training classes, but we just haven't been able to get out much recently. Soon though," Mr Jenkins added, as he watched Buttons racing about.

"Where did you get her from?" Sophie asked, wishing she could have a beautiful chocolate-coloured dog like Buttons.

"She came from a breeder who lives over on the other side of town. I got my last two dogs from him as well, but they were golden Labradors. Buttons is the first chocolate one I've had."

"Buttons is such a brilliant name for a chocolate Labrador," Sophie told him, giggling.

"Ah, that wasn't me. It was my granddaughter Phoebe's idea. She thought it was really funny."

"Does she live round here?" Sophie asked. "I don't know anyone called Phoebe at school."

"No." Mr Jenkins shook his head, sadly. "My son had to move with work earlier in the year. They live in Scotland now. I try and get up to see them, but I do miss her."

Sophie nodded. "That's sad. My grandad lives in France; we don't see him much either. And my nan and my other grandad live in London, ages away. We phone them lots, but it isn't the same as seeing them, is it?"

Mr Jenkins sighed. "Not at all. Phoebe hasn't even seen Buttons yet; I got her six weeks ago. I've sent some photos."

Buttons was enjoying following all

the delicious smells, and with Sophie holding her lead, she could go as fast as she liked. She was sure that there had been a mouse along here recently. It had gone this way, stopped here, then doubled back over here – oh! She was almost at the water's edge. She stepped back, whining. She loved to look at the water, but she didn't want to be in it.

Buttons looked up gratefully at Sophie, who was gripping her lead tightly. She was very glad that Sophie had been there to pull her out before. She knew she shouldn't have run off from Mr Jenkins like that, but they'd been going so slowly. Still she wouldn't do it again, it was far too dangerous. She wouldn't run away ever again...

Chapter Three

Sophie and the boys said goodbye to Mr Jenkins at the door. The old man was very grateful, and told Sophie that she was quick-thinking and helpful, and she reminded him of his granddaughter.

"That's all right," Sophie said, blushing, as she took her bike back from Tom. "I'm glad I was there to catch her."

Sophie watched as Mr Jenkins let himself and Buttons into the house, then she and the boys pedalled home excitedly.

Luckily Mum and Dad were having a break from painting, so they were able to listen to Sophie when she dashed in, full of her news.

"Well done, Sophie." Her dad smiled, but then he looked worried. "I hope you were careful, though. A big dog like a Labrador could've easily pulled you in, too."

"Oh no, Dad, Buttons is only little – she's just a puppy," Sophie explained. Then she noticed that Michael and Tom were making faces at her behind Dad's back and added, "And Tom and Mike were only a bit ahead of me; they'd have pulled me out if I *had* fallen in."

Her mum shuddered. "Well, thank goodness you didn't."

"I think Soph deserves an ice cream for being clever," her dad put in. "I could do with one too, after all that painting. Want to run down to the shop?"

"Oooh, yes!" And Sophie gave him a hug, carefully minding the painty bits.

When they were all sitting round in the garden eating their ice creams, Sophie said thoughtfully, "Mum, do you think Mr Jenkins would like me to walk Buttons for him while his leg's bad? He said he'd have to take it easy for a couple more days, but I think a dog like Buttons needs proper walks *every* day."

Mum and Dad exchanged glances,

and Mum sighed. "You're right, Sophie. She would need lots of walks, a young energetic dog like that. Probably Mr Jenkins could do with some help. But it's tricky. We don't want to make him feel like we're interfering, or that we think he can't cope. If he asked, it would be different…"

"I bet he won't ask," Tom said, through a mouthful of ice cream. "He's not that sort of person."

"Well, if I see him, I'll try and sound him out," Mum suggested. "OK? A compromise."

Sophie nodded reluctantly. Poor Buttons. It looked like she was going to be stuck in the garden again for a while.

Buttons followed Mr Jenkins into the house a little sadly. It had been fun walking with Sophie. Buttons tried hard not to pull on her lead with Mr Jenkins; she could tell it was hard for him to walk. She forgot sometimes, that was all. It was hard to remember to be careful when she smelled something yummy, or saw something she just had to chase. With Sophie, she had felt it was all right to be her bouncy puppy self and Buttons hoped she would see her again soon. Maybe Mr Jenkins would take her on a walk tomorrow.

But he didn't. On Monday morning, Buttons hopefully brought him her lead, just in case, but he was sitting in his chair, recovering from the effort of getting down the stairs.

"I'm sorry, Buttons. Not today."
He sighed as he took her lead and
heaved himself up. "You go and have a
run round the garden, there's a good
girl. And I'll put your food down for
you in a minute."

Buttons could feel him watching her
as she skittered off down the garden.
He looked anxious, and she wondered
what was wrong. He was holding her
lead still, and looking at it sadly.

Buttons looked around the garden and gave a little whine. She would much prefer a walk, but the garden was better than nothing. She was sniffing thoughtfully through the flower bed by the fence, when she came across a little hole under a bush. It was just large enough to get her nose into, but the loose dirt made her back out quickly, sneezing and shaking her muzzle.

Once she'd stopped pawing at her nose, Buttons sat and looked at the hole, with her head on one side. It was only a small hole. But she was quite sure it could be bigger. If there was a hole under the fence, she could go off for a walk by herself. Without even her lead! Buttons crouched down, and started to scrape at the earth with one paw...

The hole took a while to dig, but no one noticed what Buttons was doing because of the bush. It was a perfect cover.

Late the next afternoon, Buttons wriggled and squirmed her way out under the fence, and stood in the street, looking round in delight. She could explore! She could go wherever she wanted! She sniffed the air eagerly. Which way should she go first? The most delicious smells wafted past her and she pattered off down the street, looking around curiously.

On a wall two doors down from Mr Jenkins's house, a black cat was snoozing in the sun, its tail dangling invitingly down the side of the wall. Buttons trotted up to it and barked. She'd been shut up in the garden for ages and she wanted to run. It would be even better if she could chase something! She didn't know that chasing cats wasn't allowed – there was just something about the cat that made her want to bark at it...

The cat woke up with a start, and mewed frantically, its tail puffing out and all the fur standing up along its back.

Buttons stood at the bottom of the wall, barking excitedly, and the cat hissed and spat.

"Go away! Bad dog!" A woman was hurrying down the garden path, waving a trowel crossly.

Buttons didn't know what she'd done wrong, but she knew what bad dog meant. She slunk away with her tail between her legs, just in time to see Mr Jenkins standing at his gate, looking around for her worriedly.

"Is this your dog?" the cat's owner demanded. "She's been terrorizing my poor Felix. You should keep her shut up properly!"

"I'm sorry." Mr Jenkins limped out and caught Buttons by the collar. "I don't know how she got out. Has she hurt the cat?"

"Well, no," the lady admitted. "But he's terrified!" And she stomped back round the side of her house, carrying Felix and muttering about badly-behaved dogs.

"Oh, Buttons." Mr Jenkins sighed.

Buttons looked up at him apologetically, giving her tail a hopeful little wag. She hadn't been that naughty, had she?

Mr Jenkins didn't know about the hole Buttons had dug under the fence. He thought that the postman must have let her out, or the boy delivering the local paper. He put a notice on the gate reminding people to shut it carefully, and kept Buttons in for the rest of the day.

The next day, Sophie went out to send a postcard to Rachel. The postbox was in the next street to hers – the street where Mr Jenkins and

Buttons lived. Sophie was hoping she might see Buttons on the way; she was sure she'd heard her barking from her garden. Mr Jenkins might be in the garden, too – Mum hadn't had a chance to ask him about Sophie walking Buttons, and Sophie was tempted to ask him herself.

On her way back from sending her postcard, Sophie was just coming round the corner towards Mr Jenkins's house, when she heard a scuffling noise, loud barking and someone shouting.

Sophie hurried round the corner. Buttons was out! The little brown dog was standing with her front paws on the wall, barking at a black cat who was perched on the top, hissing and trying to claw at Buttons's nose.

"Oh, Buttons, no!" Sophie cried, running over. "You mustn't chase cats!"

The black cat jumped from the wall into the safety of a tree. Buttons barked one last flurry of barks, then looked guiltily at Sophie. She'd been told off about this yesterday, but she'd forgotten. Cats were just so tempting!

"Do you know this dog? Can you grab her collar, please?" A woman was hurrying up the garden path. "I need to take her back to her owner. This is the third time she's chased my cat; she was out this morning as well."

Sophie caught hold of Buttons's collar, and patted her gently to try and calm her down. Buttons wriggled, so Sophie picked her up instead, and the puppy snuggled gratefully into her arms.

"Be careful!" the cat's owner said anxiously. "She's snappy! Vicious little thing."

Sophie looked at the woman in surprise. Buttons? Sophie was sure she wasn't vicious, just a bit naughty.

The woman came out of her garden, looking worriedly up at her cat, and opened Mr Jenkins's gate. "Would you be able to take her back? She seems to behave for you. I really need to talk to Mr Jenkins, this is getting silly."

Sophie followed her, almost wishing she hadn't gone out to send her postcard. She was glad she'd been able to catch Buttons – the little dog could have been hurt if she'd run into the road – but she didn't want to be in the middle of an argument between Mr Jenkins and his neighbour.

Mr Jenkins answered the door, and he looked horrified when he saw them. "Mrs Lane! Sophie! Oh, Buttons, not again…"

"Again," Mrs Lane said grimly. "The third time. You promised me this morning you wouldn't let her out!"

"I really am sorry, Mrs Lane. I've

got someone coming to block up the hole under the fence later on, and I've kept Buttons shut in ever since I found it. She must've climbed out of the window." He gestured at an open window, and Sophie noticed that the flowers underneath looked rather squashed.

"If this happens again, I'll have to report you to the council," Mrs Lane said crossly. Then she sighed. "I'm sorry, I don't mean to be rude. But you're just not keeping her properly under control. She's a little terror!"

Mr Jenkins frowned. "I can only apologize, and promise you that it won't happen again." He sighed and leaned wearily against the door frame.

"Please make sure that it doesn't."

Mrs Lane looked at him and her voice softened. "Are you all right, Mr Jenkins? Would you like me to call your doctor? You really don't look very well."

Mr Jenkins stood up very straight. "I'm perfectly fine, thank you," he said coldly. "Sophie, could you pass Buttons to me, please?"

Sophie handed Buttons over a little reluctantly. Mrs Lane was right – he didn't look well, and she was worried Buttons was too heavy for him to carry. But she didn't dare say so. "Bye, Mr Jenkins; bye, Buttons," she whispered.

Mrs Lane stalked back down the path, and Sophie followed her, looking back to see Mr Jenkins closing the window to a tiny crack, and Buttons standing next to him now, with her paws on the window sill – Sophie guessed the puppy was standing on a chair – staring sadly after her. "See you soon, Buttons!" she whispered. Maybe next time she'd ask about being allowed to walk her.

That night, Sophie sat curled up in bed, staring out of her window. Her room was at the back of the house, and she could see the big tree in Mr Jenkins's garden and his house beyond. Buttons was in there. At least, Sophie hoped she was. She'd been lying in bed, thinking about how she'd go and see Mr Jenkins tomorrow and ask him about walking Buttons, but then she'd had an awful thought.

What if the little dog had already got out again? Sophie had a horrible feeling that if Buttons could dig one hole under the fence, then it wouldn't be long before she'd make another one. And this time she'd be in *real* trouble.

I should have been brave enough to ask Mr Jenkins about walking her, she thought miserably, one tear trickling slowly down her cheek. If Buttons didn't get walked, she'd keep trying to go out by herself. That grumpy lady had said she'd call the council if Buttons chased her cat again.

"Sophie! Why are you still awake? It's really late." Her mum was looking round the door. "Oh, Sophie, what's wrong?" She came in and sat on the end of the bed. "You're crying!"

"Mum, what would happen to a dog if somebody called the council about her?" Sophie asked worriedly.

Her mum put an arm round her shoulders. "I – I don't know, Sophie. Is this about Buttons?" Sophie had told her what had happened earlier on.

"Mrs Lane said she'd call the council. They'd take Buttons away from Mr Jenkins, Mum, I know they would. She'd get put in the dogs' home."

Her mum sighed. "I know it's hard to accept, but that might not be a bad thing…"

"Mum!" Sophie looked shocked.

"You've been saying that Mr Jenkins can't walk Buttons enough, Sophie. She's only going to get bigger, and stronger. She's not an old man's dog. She's such a sweet little thing, she'd probably be adopted by a lovely family."

"But she loves Mr Jenkins!" Sophie

told her anxiously. "You can see from the way she looks at him. And he's really lonely, with all his family so far away. He needs her, Mum." She didn't add that if Buttons got a new home, she'd never see her again – it seemed really selfish. But she couldn't help *thinking* it.

Sophie's mum nodded sadly. "I know. I'm sorry, Sophie. I just don't think there's a right answer to all of this." She stood up, and pulled Sophie's bedcover straight. "Try and go to sleep, OK?"

Sophie nodded. But after her mum had gone, she went back to looking out of the window, and thinking about poor Buttons, just across the garden. "Be good, Buttons!" she murmured, as she finally lay down to sleep.

Chapter Four

Buttons had just finished her breakfast, and she was playing with one of the new chew toys Mr Jenkins had got to keep her entertained, when she heard a terrible, sliding crash. She dashed into the hallway, where the noise seemed to have come from.

Mr Jenkins was lying in a crumpled heap at the bottom of the stairs.

Buttons howled in shock and fright. Her owner wasn't moving. It looked as though he'd tripped over his stick on the way down the stairs. Miserably, she waited for him to get up.

He didn't.

After waiting for a few minutes, staring worriedly at his closed eyes and pale face, Buttons nosed him gently. Was he asleep?

Mr Jenkins groaned, and Buttons jumped back in surprise. That wasn't a good noise.

"Buttons..." he murmured. "Good girl. I'll get up in a minute. Oh..." But as he tried to move, Mr Jenkins collapsed back again, groaning. "No, I can't." He was silent for a moment, breathing fast. "Buttons, go fetch help.

Go on…" His voice died away, and his eyes closed again, as Buttons watched him anxiously.

He didn't stir, even when Buttons licked his face, very gently.

Buttons whined. He'd said to fetch help, but she wasn't sure what he meant. Sophie! She would get Sophie. Buttons was sure she would know what to do.

Buttons backed away from Mr Jenkins slowly, and looked at the front door. It was closed. She trotted down the hallway and into the kitchen. The back door was shut, too. She nudged it hopefully. Mr Jenkins had let her out first thing – perhaps he hadn't quite closed it properly? But it was shut fast, and pawing at it did nothing.

She walked back up the hallway. Mr Jenkins hadn't moved. People weren't meant to be that still. She had to get out and find Sophie! Buttons stood by the door and barked as loudly as she could, hoping that someone would come and open it for her, but no one did.

She stared at the door for a minute, then went into the living room. Buttons eyed the window.

She knew she wasn't supposed to do this. Mr Jenkins had said no, very crossly and that she must never do it again.

But what else was she supposed to do? No one had come when she called. The doors were all shut. It was the only way out, and Mr Jenkins needed help.

Buttons clambered on to the armchair and up on to the backrest, so that her front paws were on the window sill. Then she stuck her nose through the window. It was only open a crack. Mr Jenkins liked fresh air, and he always had the windows open, but he had almost shut this one because of the time she'd climbed out of the window before. But when she pushed with her nose the window opened just a crack more.

Now she could get her ears through – although it was a squeeze and it hurt. Buttons wriggled her shoulders as if she were shaking water out of her fur, and scrabbled and scrambled and finally tumbled out of the window, landing clumsily in the flower bed underneath.

She wasn't excited by the idea of a trip, like she'd been yesterday. Now she wanted to be curled up next to Mr Jenkins's armchair, his hand stroking her ears, watching one of those delicious food programmes on the television.

Buttons headed for her little hole under the fence, but when she wriggled under the bush, it wasn't there! She lay there staring at the fence, whimpering in confusion. Brand-new boards had been nailed across the bottom, and her hole had been completely blocked up. She'd gone through all that trouble to get into the garden, and now she couldn't get out.

Suddenly Buttons's ears pricked up. She could hear Sophie! Sophie was in her garden on the other side of the back fence. She wriggled out from under the bush, barking loudly as she ran to the other end of the garden.

"Hi, Buttons!" Sophie called back, laughing, and Buttons barked louder. Sophie didn't understand! She thought Buttons was just barking to be friendly, like she sometimes did. She would have to get out of the garden and go and get Sophie. She gave a few more loud barks, then scampered back to look at the gate.

She had tried to open it before, and it hadn't worked, but she had been smaller then. She would try again. She scratched at it, but nothing much happened. It shook a little, but that was all. Buttons took a few steps back and looked up. That silvery part sticking out at the top was what made it open, she was sure. It clicked and rattled when people came in. If she could pull it across, the gate would open. And she thought she was tall enough now, if she really stretched.

Luckily for Buttons, the bolt was old and loose, but not rusty, and when she dragged at it with her strong, young teeth, it slid back easily enough. The gate opened, and Buttons sat in front of it, looking out at the street in amazement. She had done it!

Now all she had to do was find Sophie.

Buttons trotted out into the street. Then she stared back at the house, one last time, hoping the front door would open, and Mr Jenkins would come out, saying he was all right now. She wouldn't even mind if he told her off for opening the gate.

But the door stayed firmly shut. Buttons looked up and down the road. She needed to find Sophie's house. Maybe she could sniff her out.

"Naughty dog!" someone shouted, and Buttons raced off. She knew that voice – the angry lady with the cat. She wanted Buttons to come back, but Buttons wasn't going to let anyone stop her now.

Buttons sped round the corner, looking back over her shoulder anxiously. No one was following. Good. She looked at the houses on either side of the road, and her tail drooped. How was she supposed to know which house was Sophie's? She was sure it had to be along here somewhere – she could feel that she'd gone in the right direction. But working out exactly which house lined up with hers was beyond her.

Perhaps she could call Sophie? She barked hopefully, then louder and louder again. Nothing happened.

Buttons sat down in the middle of the pavement and howled. She would never find Sophie.

"Buttons!"

Sophie came running along the pavement towards her, followed by Tom and Michael. "I told you I heard her barking. There *is* something wrong, I know there is. Oh no, I hope she hasn't been chasing that cat."

Buttons ran up to them, wagging her tail gratefully. She'd almost given up.

"We'd better take her back," Tom said. "Grab her collar, Sophie, we don't want her to run into the road."

But when Sophie tried to catch hold of Buttons, she backed off.

"What's the matter, Buttons?" Sophie asked, feeling confused.

"She looks upset," Michael commented. "She isn't wagging her tail any more. She isn't hurt, is she?"

Sophie crouched down and tried to

call the puppy over. "Here, Buttons, come on. Good girl." But Buttons whimpered, and looked anxiously down the street.

Sophie frowned. "I think she wants us to follow her. Come on! Show me, good dog, Buttons." And Sophie grabbed Tom and Michael by the hand and dragged them after her.

Buttons ran along in front of them, turning every few steps to check they were following.

"I hope something hasn't happened to Mr Jenkins," Michael muttered.

"What do you mean?" Sophie asked in an anxious voice.

"I can't think why else she'd be so desperate for us to follow her," Michael explained reluctantly.

"Let's go faster," said Sophie, speeding up. "He looked awful when I took Buttons back yesterday."

They reached the house, panting, and Buttons pushed open the gate. Then she ran to the door, and paced back and forth between the door and the open window, whining. *Hurry, hurry!* she tried to tell them. *Let me in! You have to help him!*

Sophie rang the bell, but she didn't really expect anyone to answer it.

Buttons barked, sounding more and more desperate, and Tom pulled out his mobile. "Do you think we should call the police?" he asked. "Or try the neighbours?"

"Shhhh!" Sophie said suddenly. "Listen. I can hear something."

Faintly, from inside the house, she could hear a voice. Even Buttons stopped barking. She listened too, and she heard Mr Jenkins saying, "Help! Buttons, are you there? Sophie, is that you?"

"He's calling for help!" Sophie gasped. She scrabbled at the door handle, her fingers slipping. She was sure it hadn't been locked when she'd brought Buttons back before.

"Not the police, an ambulance," Tom muttered, when Sophie had got the door open and he saw Mr Jenkins lying at the foot of the stairs. "Don't move him!" he called to Sophie, who was kneeling beside the old man, her hand on Buttons's collar.

"I won't," Sophie said. "Mr Jenkins, Buttons found us. Did you send her to fetch us? She's so clever, she made us follow her."

Mr Jenkins looked up at her, smiling a little. "I knew she'd get help," he whispered. "Good dog, Buttons."

And Buttons licked his cheek, very, very gently.

Chapter Five

By the time the ambulance arrived, Mr Jenkins was looking very slightly better. There was a touch of colour in his cheeks. Buttons sat next to him, watching over him and every so often licking his hand.

The ambulance men were very impressed that Buttons had fetched Sophie, Tom and Michael.

They stroked her, and said how clever she was.

Mr Jenkins smiled, and then his face fell. "Buttons! What's going to happen to her? There's no one to take her!"

"We can arrange for her to go to the shelter for you, for a while," one of the ambulance men suggested gently.

"No, no, she'd hate that…" Mr Jenkins stared at Buttons worriedly.

Buttons whimpered, not knowing what was wrong.

"Careful now," the ambulance man warned, trying to soothe the old man. "Don't upset yourself."

"Tom, can't you ring Mum and Dad?" Sophie begged. "We could take Buttons; I'm sure they'd say 'yes' if we explained what had happened."

Mr Jenkins nodded gratefully. "That would be wonderful."

Tom grabbed his phone out of his pocket. Sophie watched nervously as he explained everything to Mum. "She said to bring her back with us," he said at last, smiling. "She wasn't sure, but she said OK."

"Go with Sophie, Buttons," Mr Jenkins whispered, as the ambulance men carried his stretcher away down the path. "There's a good girl."

The ambulance sped away with its blue lights flashing, and Buttons whimpered as she stared after it, watching until it disappeared round the corner. Then she looked up trustingly at Sophie. Mr Jenkins had said to go with her, so she would.

Just at that moment, Mrs Lane, Mr Jenkins's neighbour, came hurrying down the street. She had seen the ambulance, and she looked worried.

"Oh my goodness, was that Mr Jenkins?" she asked the children, and when they nodded, she dropped her shopping bag, and her face went pale. "I knew I should have made him see a doctor," she murmured. "But he was so stubborn. Oh! The dog! What on earth are we going to do with her?"

"We're taking her home with us," Sophie said firmly.

Mrs Lane looked surprised, but rather relieved. "I can't possibly take her, you know. She chases Felix," she said very firmly.

Tom and Michael carried Buttons's things out of the house, and Sophie clipped on her lead. Mr Jenkins had said to take everything they needed, and given them his door key to lock up afterwards.

"Don't let her get out," Mrs Lane advised as she stood watching.

Sophie, Tom and Michael smiled politely, and didn't say anything, but as soon as they were round the corner – the boys laden down with baskets and bowls and Sophie holding Buttons's lead and a bag of dog food – they exchanged glances.

"She really doesn't like Buttons, does she…" Tom muttered. "I'm glad Buttons didn't get left with her. She'd have been down at the dogs' home before she could blink."

"Buttons was only getting out and being naughty because she hadn't been walked, but that wasn't Mr Jenkins's fault," Sophie said loyally.

Sophie's mum was standing at the gate watching for them. "Oh my goodness," she murmured, as she saw everything the boys were carrying. "Look at all that stuff!"

Buttons looked up at her worried face and whimpered. Everyone was cross at the moment, and Mr Jenkins had gone away and left her. She raised her head to the sky and howled.

"You'd better bring her through," Mum said, sighing.

Sophie coaxed Buttons in, and the boys carried all the things into the kitchen, putting them down next to their dad, who looked rather surprised to find a dog eyeing his sandwich enviously.

Dad shook his head, smiling a little. "Looks like you three have got your wish, even if it is only for a week or two. Because that's all it is," he added firmly. "She's going back to Mr Jenkins, so don't get too fond of her, will you?"

It was easy to promise that they wouldn't get too fond of Buttons, but Sophie adored her already and soon she couldn't imagine life without her. Having her to look after every day wasn't boring or hard work, as Dad had warned them. Tom borrowed a DVD on dog-training from the library, and Sophie and the boys started to teach her to walk, heel, sit and stay. They'd always thought of Buttons as rather a naughty dog, because whenever they saw her she'd slipped her lead or tripped someone up. When they'd first taken her for walks, Sophie had held on to her lead so carefully, convinced that Buttons would keep trying to dash off. But although she did pull at her lead a bit, she didn't run away at all. And she was brilliant at the obedience training.

"Labradors are very clever," Dad said, after he'd watched admiringly as they put Buttons through her paces for him. She'd even sat for a whole minute with a dog biscuit between her paws, until Sophie told her she was allowed to eat it.

Buttons was happy, too. She had been very confused that first day, with a new house and a new garden and new people, even if her own basket and her bowls were there. And to start with she had missed Mr Jenkins terribly. Everywhere smelled different and strange, and she followed Sophie around as though she was glued to her.

On Saturday night, Mum had looked at her sad little face and big, round black eyes, and sighed. "I suppose she's going to have to sleep in your room, Sophie. But not on your bed!" she added, as Sophie rushed to hug her.

Although Buttons still thought about Mr Jenkins, she was so happy living with a family who had as much energy as she did. It was the walks that made things so different. An early-morning quick run before breakfast with Sophie. Sometimes a trip down to the shops during the day. And then a proper long walk later on. Up to the common, or along the canal bank. On the Saturday a week after she'd come home with them, the whole family went in the car to a big wood a few miles from the town, and Buttons had a blissful time chasing imaginary rabbits.

That evening when they got home, Sophie sent Rachel an email. She had to type rather slowly, with Buttons sitting on her lap and staring curiously at the computer.

```
To: Rachel
From: Sophie                    📎 Attachment:
Subject: Our new dog?             Buttons.jpg

Hi Rache!
You'll never guess, we've got a dog!
She's called Buttons, and she's so
cute. I wish you could see her for
real, but I took a photo of her when
we went to the woods today so here it
is. We're only looking after her
while her owner's in hospital, but
she feels like she's actually ours.
```

Sophie stopped typing, and stroked Buttons's soft ears. It was true. Buttons did feel like her dog. "You're the nicest dog I've ever met, do you know that?" she whispered to her, and Buttons turned round and licked her nose lavishly. Sophie giggled, and made *yeeuchh* noises, but really she'd never been happier.

Chapter Six

Sophie had made her mum phone the hospital every day to see how Mr Jenkins was, and to pass on messages about how well Buttons was doing. Mr Jenkins had had to have an operation on his leg, but he was getting better quickly, and the nurses told her that he could have visitors. They even suggested that Sophie, Michael and Tom came, saying that he talked about them all the time and how clever they'd been to rescue him. Mr Jenkins's son had rung the Martins to say how grateful he was to them for looking after Buttons. He begged them to visit too, as he wasn't able to stay away from his family in Scotland for very long, and he was worried that his dad was lonely in the hospital.

So on Monday, just over a week after Mr Jenkins's accident, Sophie and Tom and their mum knocked on the door of Mr Jenkins's room. Luckily it was on the ground floor, as Michael was still outside – with Buttons.

Mr Jenkins was sitting up in bed, reading a newspaper and looking very bored, but he threw it down delightedly when he saw them.

"You came to see me!" he exclaimed. "Is Buttons all right?" he asked eagerly, and Sophie and Tom grinned at each other. Mum had checked with the nurses, and they'd said it was all right to move his bed closer to the window.

"We've got a surprise!" Sophie explained, as she helped to push the bed to the window. "Look!"

Just outside the window was Michael. Except they couldn't really see him, because he was holding Buttons up in front of his face. She wriggled and woofed delightedly as soon as she saw her owner, and tried to lick the glass.

"Oh, I wish we could bring her in," Sophie said sadly. "She's so pleased to see you."

"You've looked after her so well," Mr Jenkins said, smiling. "I can't wait to be out of this place and have her back home with me."

Sophie nodded and smiled, but his words made her feel sick. How could she go back to only seeing Buttons when she walked past Mr Jenkins's garden? She couldn't bear it, after having Buttons almost for her own.

Sophie had known all along that Buttons would have to go home again. But the gorgeous puppy felt like a part of the family now. It was going to be so hard to give her up. She could tell from looking at Mr Jenkins how happy he was to see Buttons. The little dog was all the company he had, now his family had moved away. But Sophie felt like she needed Buttons too. And Buttons needed owners who could give her all the exercise a bouncy young dog had to have. It was so hard.

Sophie was very silent all the way home, and then she took Buttons up to her room (she wasn't supposed to have her on the bed, but Mum pretended not to notice the hairs). Sophie stroked the puppy's velvety ears, and sighed.

Buttons looked at Sophie, her head on one side, her dark eyes sparkling. She gave a hopeful little bark, and nudged her rubber bone towards her. Sometimes they played a really good game where Sophie pretended to pull the bone away, and Buttons pretended to do fierce growling. But maybe Sophie didn't want to play that today.

Sophie tickled her under the chin, and Buttons closed her eyes and whined with pleasure. Sophie knew just where to scratch.

Sophie sniffed back tears. "I can't give you back," she whispered. "I just can't." But she knew she would have to soon.

"Do you really think we can?" Sophie asked excitedly.

Tom nodded. "I think so. She's so good now. We've been training her to walk to heel and stay for nearly a month. Anyway, the common's not too busy today, so hopefully she won't be tempted to dash off and see any other dogs."

"And we've worn her out a good bit already," Michael pointed out.

"OK then." Sophie knelt down next to Buttons, who was sitting, panting happily with her tongue hanging out. It had been a long, hot walk up to the highest point of the common. Sophie's heart started to thump a little as she slipped the catch on Buttons's lead.

How would she react?

Buttons looked round in surprise. Then she gave a pleased little woof, but she didn't make a run for it, as Sophie had dreaded she would. She gazed up at Sophie, as though she was checking Sophie had really meant to let her off the lead. Then she trotted off a few metres, found an enormous stick and dragged it back. She dropped it at Tom's feet, and barked pleadingly at him.

"She wants to play fetch!" Sophie exclaimed. "We haven't even taught her that. I told you she was clever!"

"You couldn't find anything smaller?" Tom pretended to complain, but he flung the stick as far as he could, and Buttons chased after it, barking delightedly.

They played fetch for ages, then walked home, all tired but happy.

Mum was in the kitchen, stirring her coffee round and round, and looking sad.

"What's wrong?" Sophie asked. She had a horrible feeling she already knew.

Mum smiled. "Oh, it's good news, really. Mr Jenkins came home from hospital yesterday. He's much better, and he asked if we could bring Buttons home." She waved a hand at the counter, which was piled up with Buttons's bowls, and the toys Sophie and the boys had bought her. "I've got everything ready. We just need to put it all in her basket."

Sophie slumped into a chair, and Tom and Michael leaned up against the counter, all staring at the sad little pile.

"I can't believe she's going," Michael muttered.

"We just got her to come when she was called. We even let her off the lead today," Tom said flatly.

"I know it's hard, but we always knew she wasn't really our dog…" Mum started. Then she sighed. "No, I can't pretend I won't miss her dreadfully too."

Dad came in from the garden. "You told them then?" he murmured, seeing everyone's miserable faces. "I'm sorry, you lot, but I told Mr Jenkins we'd be round some time this afternoon."

Sophie's eyes filled with tears, as she watched Dad pick up Buttons's basket and start to pack the dog bowls into it.

Dad put the basket down, and came to give Sophie a hug. "You knew it wasn't for always, Sophie. And you'll still be able to see her. I bet Mr Jenkins would love you to visit."

Sophie gulped and nodded, and Buttons nudged her affectionately, licking her hand. She wanted Sophie to cheer up, and come and play in the garden. They could do more of the fetching game, with a ball this time. But Sophie was reaching down to clip her lead back on. Buttons gave her a surprised look. Another walk? Well, that was wonderful, but right now? She was quite tired. She'd been planning to have a good long drink before she did anything else, but her water bowl seemed to have disappeared.

"Come on, Buttons!" Sophie said, trying to sound cheerful. She led the dreary little parade out of the front door.

Buttons's tail started to wag delightedly as they walked up the path to Mr Jenkins's front door.

"See, she's happy to be back," Dad said firmly.

Sophie gulped. She wanted Buttons to be happy, didn't she? It would be horrible if she was upset as well. But all the same … didn't Buttons love them at all? Wouldn't she miss them, too?

Buttons waited for the door to open, her tail swinging back and forth so hard it beat against Sophie's legs. Mr Jenkins's house! Her old house! She was going to see her old owner.

That was what he was now. Her old

owner. She belonged to Sophie these days, and Michael and Tom. But it would still be good to see him.

When the door opened, she tried to fling herself against Mr Jenkins's legs, and lick him all over, but Sophie said, "Down, Buttons! Gently!" and she sat back at once. Of course. She had to be careful with Mr Jenkins. She padded calmly into the hallway, and let Sophie unclip her lead.

"You've done wonders with her," Mr Jenkins said admiringly. "She's so much calmer. She's like a different dog. I just can't thank you enough."

"She's been really good," Sophie said, her voice tight. "And it was fun training her."

Mr Jenkins offered to make them all

tea, but Dad said no, they didn't want to make work for him when he was only just back. Really he wanted to get Sophie and the boys home before Sophie burst into tears.

Buttons watched in surprise as Dad fetched her basket from the hallway and put it down in Mr Jenkins's living room. That was her basket. She would need it. Why were they leaving it here? Then at last she understood, and she whimpered, staring up at Sophie.

"You're home now, Buttons," Sophie said in a very small, shaky voice. She was holding back her tears. "You're going to look after Mr Jenkins, aren't you?" She crouched down to stroke Buttons's nose, and whispered, "Please don't forget us!" in her ear.

Then they left, and Buttons stared after them out of the window. She remembered now that it was her special job to look after her old owner. But she wished she could go home with Sophie.

Chapter Seven

With no Buttons, it felt like there was a hole in the house. She wasn't jumping hopefully round while the Martins got ready to go out, begging with her enormous eyes for them to take her, too. She wasn't there barking with delight when they got home again. She wasn't sitting under the table during meals, her nose wedged lovingly on someone's knee, waiting for crumbs or the odd toast crust. She wasn't on Sophie's bed at night, so Sophie could burrow her toes underneath her warm weight. She was gone.

The summer days stretched out emptily with no dog to walk. Everyone moped around the house, until Mum and Dad sat the children down to talk one morning, just a few days after they'd taken Buttons back.

"Look, I know you all miss Buttons," Dad told them gently. "We had her for nearly a month, long enough for it to feel like she was ours. But try and think of it like this. You did such a good job looking after her, and now she's back where she belongs. Mr Jenkins needs her more than we do – she's all he's got.

We're really proud of you, you know. Especially all that hard work you put into training her." He smiled at their mum, and she nodded. "So we were thinking, maybe it's time we let you have a dog of your own." He sat back and looked at them hopefully, but no one said anything. And then Sophie got up from the table and ran out of the room.

"She only wants Buttons," Michael muttered.

Dad nodded sadly. "I guess it might be a bit too soon. But I mean it, boys. You all did well. And you deserve a dog of your own, when you're ready for one."

That weekend, Dad loaded them all into the car, and refused to tell the children where they were going. "It's a secret," he said, smiling at their mum.

They drove through the town, and Sophie and Michael and Tom tried to work out where they were heading, but Dad wouldn't say if they were right.

Then suddenly Sophie gasped. "The shelter! We're going to the dogs' home, aren't we?" Her voice shook, and she was choking up as she went on. "Please don't, Dad. I don't want to look at other dogs."

"Hey, come on, Sophie, let's just go and see," Tom said excitedly. "Is she right, Dad? Are we going to the shelter?"

"Yup." Dad pulled up close to a big blue sign that said *Rushbrook Animal Shelter*. "And we're here. Come on, everyone."

"Remember we're just looking at the moment," Mum warned the boys, as she walked in with her arm round Sophie, who was trying really hard not to cry.

"We know!" Michael promised, but he and Tom were racing ahead, eager to see all the dogs they were imagining could be theirs.

"I hope this wasn't a bad idea," Mum murmured.

The shelter was full, and all the dogs looked desperate for new homes. Even though Sophie hated the thought of getting another dog – it would feel like she had forgotten Buttons – she had to read the cards over the pens. And once she knew the dogs' names, and their stories, she couldn't help caring about them a little bit.

"Oh, Sophie, look..." Mum was crouching next to the wire front of a pen, gazing at a greyhound, whose long legs were spilling out of his basket. "He's lovely, isn't he? Not that we could get a greyhound, they must need so much exercise. Look at his legs!"

"Actually it says here that older

greyhounds don't like too much exercise. They're quite lazy. He's called Fred and he's looking for a quiet, loving home." Sophie looked at Fred, snoozing happily. "He looks pretty relaxed," she said, giggling.

"Oh, it's nice to see you smile!" Her mum hugged her. "Sophie, you know, even if you don't want a dog now, I'm sure you will one day. You were so wonderful with Buttons."

"That's because she was wonderful," Sophie whispered, digging her nails into her palms so as not to start crying again. "Sorry, Mum." She sniffed hard, and turned back to look at Fred. "He does look lovely, though," she said bravely.

Michael and Tom wanted about six different dogs each, but on the way home in the car even they had to agree that the perfect dog hadn't been at the shelter this time. "But they said they get new dogs all the time, Dad," Tom pointed out. "Can we go back soon?" Sophie leaned against the window and closed her eyes. She wasn't sure she could bear to go again. All those gorgeous dogs, all wanting a home and someone to love them. But Sophie just couldn't love another dog. Not yet.

At Mr Jenkins's house, Buttons was moping, too. She tried not to show it, but it was so hard going back to little short walks. Mr Jenkins was much, much better since his operation, but he still had a stick, and he couldn't walk fast, or for very long. There were no more fantastic runs over the common. No imaginary rabbit-hunting in the woods. Just slow, gentle ambles round the streets. Mr Jenkins couldn't help noticing on their walks that his bouncy, overexcited little puppy had turned into a sad young dog instead. He was glad that she was so well-behaved, of course − Sophie and her brothers had done wonders with her − but he almost wished that just occasionally she would be her silly, happy little self again.

Buttons was very good. She walked to heel, like Tom and Michael and Sophie had shown her. She wondered if Mr Jenkins would let her off the lead, so she could fetch, but she supposed he didn't know she could do that now. She never tried to get out of the garden, even though she could have done, if she'd wanted. She knew how to open the bolt after all. She looked at it sometimes, and wondered about going to see Sophie. But she wasn't supposed to. She didn't belong there any more.

Chapter Eight

Sophie's mum put down the phone, and came slowly back to the table, where everyone was finishing lunch.

"Who was that?" Sophie asked.

"It was Mr Jenkins. He's asked us all round for a cup of tea this afternoon." Mum looked at Sophie, whose face had suddenly crumpled, and Tom and Michael, and said firmly, "I told him of course we would love to. It will be nice to see him."

Sophie stared at her fruit salad, and knew she couldn't eat any more. "Please may I leave the table," she muttered, getting up. She wasn't sure she could be brave enough to go and see Buttons in her real home. Not when she kept imagining her back here.

Her mum sighed and let Sophie go. She looked worriedly at their dad. "It's going to be especially hard for Sophie to see Buttons. She hasn't been in the garden when we've walked past, and I've been grateful. But I suppose it has to happen sooner or later."

Sophie trailed behind the others as they went round to Mr Jenkins's house, walking as slowly as she could. She was desperate to see Buttons, of course she was. And she felt guilty about not going to visit Mr Jenkins sooner.

But she hadn't been able to make herself go. It had been two whole weeks, and she was only just starting to miss Buttons a tiny bit less. If she saw her again, Sophie knew it would be worse than before.

Mr Jenkins answered the door, and there was Buttons, tail wagging furiously, gazing up at Sophie, her big, brown eyes full of love. Sophie had to look away. But she made herself look back and smile. She didn't want Buttons to be miserable too.

Mr Jenkins sent them all to sit down while he made tea and got juice, and then he asked Tom to carry the tray in for him. He seemed a lot better, although he still had his stick. Buttons stayed right next to him the whole time, so when he sat down she sat by him, but she stared at Sophie.

Sophie stared back, sadly.

Buttons edged slightly closer, wriggling on her bottom to where Sophie was sitting next to her mum on the sofa. She wanted to cheer Sophie up. She could try, at least. Inch by inch, she travelled the short distance to the sofa, and leaned her nose lovingly against Sophie's leg.

Sophie stroked her, her eyes filling with tears. "Oh, I've really missed you," she whispered to Buttons. Then she realized that Mr Jenkins was talking, now that he'd made sure everyone had a drink. He sounded very serious.

"I need to ask you all an enormous favour." He looked at Buttons, her head in Sophie's lap, and sighed. "All the time I was in the hospital, I was so keen to be at home, back to normal, with my dog. The same as things were before. But since I've been back home I've realized that what I suspected was right. I wasn't looking after Buttons well enough before. I can't keep up with her!" He smiled sadly. "It's going to be a huge wrench – I've always had a dog, always had big dogs – but I'm going to have to give her up. I couldn't even manage to train her properly!"

He looked at Tom and Michael and Sophie, who were staring back at him wide-eyed. "You three did what I just didn't have the energy to do – turned Buttons into a beautifully behaved dog. Since she's been back with me, she hasn't pulled on her lead, she hasn't barged into me. She's been a treasure. But it isn't fair on her, having to live with a doddery old man. She needs to be able to go racing up to the common. So I've decided. She's going to have to go to the shelter. Unless…"

Sophie gulped.

Mr Jenkins smiled at her. "Unless you can take her. I mean, keep her. Have her as yours. She's missed you, you know. Every time she goes into the garden, she goes and stands by the back fence. She's listening out for you in your garden."

Sophie looked up at her mum, her eyes pleading, and saw that she was laughing.

"We'd told the children they could have their own dog, because they'd looked after Buttons so well. We even went to the shelter to look for one. But none of us could find the dog we wanted, we missed Buttons so much. Of course we'll have her!"

Sophie slipped off the sofa, and hugged Buttons round the neck. "You're coming home with us, Buttons! You're really our dog now!" Then she looked up at Mr Jenkins, frowning. "But what will you do without her? Won't you miss her?"

Mr Jenkins nodded. "Of course I will. But it isn't fair to make her miserable, just to keep me happy."

"I could bring her to see you..." Sophie suggested, and Mr Jenkins smiled gratefully.

They finished their tea, and Mr Jenkins found all Buttons's things for them to take home. He was trying to be cheerful, but Sophie could see he was really upset about giving Buttons away. He was going to be so lonely without her.

Sophie was watching him stroke Buttons lovingly as they said goodbye, when it suddenly came to her.

"Oh! I've just had the most brilliant idea! When we went to the shelter, there was a greyhound, a gorgeous brindled one, called Fred. The card on his pen said he was quite old, and he wanted a quiet, loving home! That's you!"

Mr Jenkins stared at her, frowning thoughtfully as he leaned against the doorframe. "A greyhound ... I've never had a greyhound before. I hadn't thought of going to the shelter, but they do want homes for older dogs, don't they..." He smiled. "Do you think you and Buttons would let an old man and an old dog tag along on your walks sometimes, Sophie?"

Buttons looked up at Sophie's glowing face, and Mr Jenkins's smile, and even though she stood beautifully still, her tail waved joyfully. Buttons could see they were happy and she was, too – she was going home.

The Brave Kitten

From best-selling author
HOLLY WEBB

Helena loves helping out at the vet's surgery where her older cousin Lucy works. When they find a young cat who's been injured by a car, they take him straight there. Helena helps to care for the cat she calls Caramel, but when it's time for him to go home, Caramel's owner can't be traced.

Caramel is fed-up with being kept at the surgery and he especially doesn't like the scratchy bandage on his leg. But if no one comes forward to claim him, how will he ever have a place to call home?

The Forgotten Puppy

From best-selling author
HOLLY WEBB

Emi has wanted a dog for as long as she can remember. So when she gets Rina, a little Shiba Inu puppy, Emi wants to take her everywhere. There's just one problem – she has to leave Rina behind on the weekends she spends with Dad.

Rina can't understand why Emi keeps going away! When one of the trips seems longer than usual, she's convinced that Emi has forgotten all about her. Rina sets off to find her owner. But where should she look?

The Secret Kitten

Special
edition
30th
Animal
Story

From best-selling author
HOLLY WEBB

Moving to a new house and school is hard for Lucy. Then she finds a family of stray kittens in an alleyway, and doesn't feel quite so lonely. She especially lovesthe shy black-and-white one, and calls her Catkin.

Catkin doesn't like it when the other kittens are taken away. Then Lucy makes her a new home in their greenhouse. But the kitten can't stay there forever. Just how long can Lucy keep Catkin a secret?

A Home for Molly

From best-selling author
HOLLY WEBB

Anya has been worried about feeling
lonely on holiday with only her baby
sister to play with. So she is delighted
when she meets some new friends
on the beach. And when a gorgeous
puppy, Molly, joins in their games
it looks like this could be the best
summer ever!

It's been such a long time since Molly
had an owner. Then she meets Anya
and she doesn't feel so alone any more.
But will Anya be able to give Molly the
home she's been looking for?

HOLLY WEBB

Holly Webb started out as a children's book editor, and wrote her first series for the publisher she worked for. She has been writing ever since, with over one hundred books to her name. Holly lives in Berkshire, with her husband and three young sons. Holly's pet cats are always nosying around when she is trying to type on her laptop.

For more information
about Holly Webb visit:

www.holly-webb.com